BAND ROOM BASH

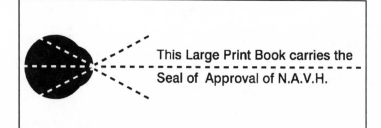

This Large Print Book carries the
Seal of Approval of N.A.V.H.

MAYHEM IN MARYLAND, BOOK TWO

BAND ROOM BASH

A ROMANTIC MYSTERY

CANDICE SPEARE

THORNDIKE PRESS
A part of Gale, Cengage Learning

GALE
CENGAGE Learning·

Detroit • New York • San Francisco • New Haven, Conn • Waterville, Maine • London

GALE
CENGAGE Learning

Copyright © 2008 by Candice Speare.
Scripture quotations are taken from the Holy Bible, New International Version®. NIV®. Copyright © 1973, 1978, 1984 by International Bible Society. Used by permission of Zondervan. All rights reserved.
Thorndike Press, a part of Gale, Cengage Learning.

LIBRARY OF CONGRESS CATALOGING-IN-PUBLICATION DATA

Speare, Candice.
    Band room bash : a romantic mystery / by Candice Speare.
        p. cm. — (Mayhem in Maryland ; bk. 2) (Thorndike Press large print Christian mystery)
    ISBN-13: 978-1-4104-2139-5 (hardcover : alk. paper)
    ISBN-10: 1-4104-2139-2 (hardcover : alk. paper) 1.
Housewives—Fiction. 2. Teachers—Crimes against—Fiction. 3. Murder—Investigation—Fiction. 4. Suburban life—Maryland—Fiction. 5. Large type books. I. Title.
PS3619.P3735B36 2010
813'.6—dc22
                                      2009038131

Published in 2010 by arrangement with Barbour Publishing, Inc.

I'm grateful to the following people, without whom this book would never have made it from my brain to the paper. Brad, who knew I could do it again. My mom who brainstormed the ending with me . . . over and over and over again. My editor and friend Susan Downs for all her encouragement and support. My family for being there — always. Joyce and Nancy, who spent a hectic week critiquing the final version. Ellen Tarver, content and line editor extraordinaire. And Scot Hopkins, a twenty-year law enforcement veteran who generously shared his time and expertise, saving me from making embarrassing police procedural errors. (If there are any mistakes of any kind, be they grammatical or procedural, I take full responsibility because that means I wasn't paying close enough attention to what people told me.)

1

This is developing into a very bad habit!
I don't know if I can explain it to you.
It's not only against the law, it's wrong.
— Mortimer Brewster in
Arsenic and Old Lace

No matter how old I get, when I stand in front of the doors of Four Oaks High School, I have flashbacks. Like today, the crisp fall air reminded me of playing in the marching band during halftime. Of course, the good memories are interspersed with memories of rampaging insecurities — something I still struggle with.

I yanked open the doors and turned my focus to my reason for being here — a committee meeting about *Arsenic and Old Lace,* a play in which Tommy, my teenage stepson, had a role. Somehow, I'd been coerced into collecting advertising from local merchants for the play program. Not that I resented doing things for my kids, but I was eight months pregnant and feeling slightly irritable because I'd originally taken off the afternoon to prepare for a romantic evening alone with my husband.

I headed down the locker-lined hall toward the end of the building where I was supposed to meet the other committee members in the band room. When I rounded a corner, I saw Carla Bickford, the school principal, walking toward me. She held a clipboard stacked with papers in one hand and a Styrofoam coffee cup in the other.

"Trish, I'm glad I caught you." Her chest moved with rapid breaths. "The play meeting has just been canceled. Marvin is feeling poorly and has to go home. We need him for this meeting. I've rescheduled for Wednesday, same time."

"That works for me." Things were looking up. Even though I'd have to take time off work again to attend the next meeting, the extra time this afternoon was a gift. I glanced at my watch. I could make it home in plenty of time to make a special dinner for my husband, sans kids.

Carla cleared her throat. "I've tried to get the message to everyone, but I could only find Marvin. He was down in the teacher's lounge getting a Coke." Her lips tightened. "I told him that was foolish. He's had indigestion for weeks. He probably has an ulcer because he's so high-strung. You never know what he's going to do next."

Her comment surprised me. Marvin was the best band director the school ever had, leading the band to honors at prestigious contests. A miracle for a small town high school. And though he'd impressed me as an intense musician, he never seemed flaky.

"I hope he's feeling better soon." I turned to go, my mind already focused on the cute black maternity dress I'd bought to entice my husband.

"Wait," Carla said. "We can't put the play program advertising on hold for two days."

I turned back around to face her. "No problem." I already had several potential contributors in mind, including our family-owned self-storage business.

"Good. Come to my office for a moment. I have some forms that I was going to give to you today. You can take them now."

I stared at Carla. "Forms?"

"Yes." She walked past me toward the front of the building. "I'd like you to get people to fill them out when they agree to advertise."

I wondered why we had to go to the

extreme of having people fill out official forms, but I said nothing, just followed her. Her gray suit fit her like a military uniform. Her broad shoulders didn't need the shoulder pads in her jacket. Everything about her was boxy, including her brown hair, which reminded me of a helmet.

In her office, Carla put the cup on a credenza. On her desk, piles of papers lay in neat rows, their edges perpendicular with the edges of the desktop. Without hesitation, she picked up one of the stacks.

"Here. You can ask one of my secretaries to make copies for you if you need more." She stretched out her arm to give them to me, and I saw a delicate gold watch on her desk.

"That's pretty." I took the papers from her hand.

She snatched it up. "It needs some work."

"Is it broken?" I asked.

"Yes." She opened her middle desk drawer and dropped the watch into it.

She frowned and opened the drawer wider. I noticed scattered pens and mechanical pencils, along with a tube of lipstick, a compact, and a couple of prescription bottles. She slammed the drawer shut.

"That's too bad. It's a very nice watch." I glanced at the forms in my hand and thumbed through the top one, thinking that a two-page agreement for a simple advertisement in a school play program was overkill.

"It's from my fiancé," she said as she picked up her phone and punched in a number.

I glanced up at her. She didn't bother with niceties when someone answered. "Have you been in my desk again?" she demanded.

I heard murmurs from the receiver in her hand.

A red flush worked up Carla's cheeks. "I know I was away. That's no excuse."

More murmurs came through the receiver.

Carla glanced at me and took a deep breath. "Well, I'll let it slide this time because you're a new employee, but I don't like anyone in my desk. It's mine."

I thought it likely Carla had never lived with children. If she had, she'd be used to having her desk and everything else in her life ransacked.

After slapping the phone down, she looked at me. "I don't understand why people can't comprehend the idea of personal property." She sniffed and pointed at the stack of forms in my hand. "I want those filled out completely."

I nodded.

Her gaze fell to my stomach. "When,

exactly, are you due?"

"In —"

"Soon," she interrupted me. "I can tell by your size." Her eyes met mine. "Are you sure you can handle the advertising?"

"Well, I —"

"A birth in the middle of planning would be detrimental, you know. This has —"

"I'm fine." Interrupting her in return was the only way I'd be able to stop her. "I have one more month. The advertising will be taken care of before the baby comes."

She raised her brows. "Well, if you're sure."

"I'm absolutely sure."

Like the job of getting advertising for a small town high school play program was the equivalent of being an ad exec for a huge corporation. I stared at the wrinkles on Carla's forehead. She'd been principal for two years. She had always been pushy, but lately her behavior reminded me of a big-wheeled monster truck at the fair, running over everything in its path.

I stood to go.

"Wait one more minute, please," she said. "I haven't been able to find Connie Gilbert to notify her about the meeting cancellation. My new secretary informed me that she was here with some sample costumes for us to look at, but I was on the phone and couldn't catch her. My secretary also said that Connie was searching for Georgia Winters. Apparently, they are quarreling."

She made a note on the top paper on her clipboard. "I don't have time to continue the search, and I don't want to get involved in their personal issues. Will you please try to find Connie for me?" She pointed at another stack of forms on her desk. "These are for her. I'd like her to pick them up today. They're forms for each of the play participants to fill out with their measurements."

The phone on her desk rang.

"I don't —"

"Thank you, Trish. Oh, and perhaps you can find Georgia, as well. Tell her to meet me in my office. We have a dinner engagement." Carla snatched up the receiver. "Yes?"

I had been dismissed. After being given orders. Well, I'd search while I looked for Tommy. Besides, as tense as Carla seemed to be, maybe this would ease some of her pressure.

Ten minutes later, after a fruitless visit to the teacher's lounge, I found Connie Gilbert in Georgia Winters's English classroom. Connie had her back to the door. There was no sign of Georgia.

"Hey, Connie."

She whirled around, body stiff, mouth in an O. Then she met my gaze and relaxed. "Trish." She held a folded piece of paper in her hand and slipped it into the pocket of her blue linen jacket.

As I walked into the room, I smelled a strong floral perfume. I wondered if it was Connie's or Georgia's. Georgia's desk was covered with papers, but unlike Carla's, everything here was a mess. A white coffee mug sat there with lipstick on the rim. A black grade book was partially covered by a paper plate on which sat a half-eaten powdered sugar doughnut. Pens and pencils overflowed a long, flowered dish.

I met Connie's gaze. "I'm on assignment to tell you that the meeting has been canceled, and Carla has some forms on her desk for you to pick up."

"Yes, Marvin told me awhile ago." She brushed a stray piece of wispy blond hair from her pale face. Her nose was pink at the end and her eyes slightly puffy. I wondered if she had a cold. Though she was on the wiry side, she had shape in the right places and was very pretty in a soft, unfocused way. Just the kind of woman men fall over themselves to help because she comes

14

across as defenseless. I'd never been able to accomplish that and was jealous of women who could.

"Are you okay?" I asked.

She nodded and bowed her head.

"So you're doing the costumes for the play?"

"Yes." She took a wool costume jacket from a box on the floor and brushed off the lapels. "I just got a bunch from someone I know who does off-Broadway," she said in her soft voice. "I think I'm going to need another storage unit. Do you guys have any available?"

I thought about the occupancy chart I'd looked at before I left Four Oaks Self-Storage that afternoon. "Yeah, I think we do have a vacancy in the building where your other units are. Just call Shirl and tell her I said to hold it for you. If you can come by tomorrow morning, we'll get you set up."

"Thank you," Connie said. "Oh, I saw Tommy earlier. He's gotten quite tall this last year. I might have to let out hems on the costumes for him."

"A seventeen-year growth spurt," I said. "How long ago did you see him? I need to give him a message."

She shrugged. "Probably about thirty minutes ago, heading for the band room."

"What about Georgia? Have you seen her?"

"No." Connie carefully folded the costume jacket and added it to a neat stack on a student desk, patting it into place. "In fact, Carla's secretary told me Carla was looking for Georgia. So was Tommy."

I frowned at her. "Why was Tommy looking for her?"

Connie picked up a shirt and folded it. "Something about a test."

I sighed, resigned that I was going to spend the next hour tracking people down. I'd start in the band room.

The band room door was closed. I grabbed the handle and pushed, expecting it to swing open. It didn't. I pushed again and met the same resistance. Something was holding the door shut.

"Hello?" I yelled. "Marvin? Are you there?"

I leaned on the door, pushing harder, and it gave enough that I could stick my hand through the crack and try to figure out what was blocking my entrance. I felt the top of a chair and tried to scoot it out of the way, but it wouldn't move. I removed my hand and jammed my face against the door, peering inside with one eye. The distinctive smell of the band room wafted out through the crack, strong in the stuffy silence. Cork grease, spit from the instruments, teenagers — I wasn't sure what created the odor, but it hadn't changed since I was a kid. Light from the afternoon sunshine coming through the windows, along with the glare of fluorescent lights on the ceiling, clearly illuminated two overturned music stands, along with scattered music next to a bassoon on the floor.

Had there been some sort of struggle? I backed up, not sure what to do. That's when I realized how alone I was. Hairs on the back of my neck prickled. I'd been so focused on finding Tommy and Georgia that I hadn't noticed the emptiness of the halls. I fumbled in my purse for my cell phone. Then I heard the thud of footsteps coming down the hall. I whirled around.

Tommy.

I let out a whoosh of air and didn't realize until that moment that I'd been holding my breath. "I was looking for you. I'm glad you're here. I can't get the band room door open."

Tommy frowned. "That's weird. Let me try."

I stepped aside. He pressed his body against the door. It didn't budge. He backed up a step for momentum then slammed into the door with all his weight. It opened enough to allow us entrance. He stepped inside and scanned the room then peered behind the door.

"Whoa."

"Whoa what?" I rushed inside, nearly tripping on the bassoon. Then I skidded to a stop.

We'd found Georgia. She was lying in the space behind the door next to the chair and a fallen music stand. The weight of her prone body must have been what held the door shut.

I swallowed hard then shook the strap of my purse off my shoulder and dropped it to the floor. "Tommy, call 911."

"Mom, you gotta be careful. Dad said to watch out for you and —"

"Thank you, but please, just call." I knelt clumsily next to Georgia, ignoring the murmurs of Tommy's voice. Blood oozed through her thick, black, shoulder-length hair, gathering in a puddle on the floor, which was drying around the edges. She had been sick — I saw remnants of that, too. Her eyes were open and sightless. I was raised on a farm. I'd seen the eyes of enough dead animals to recognize no life when I saw it. Still, I felt for a pulse.

Tommy was breathing heavily. "It's Ms. Winters," he said into the phone. "Uh, that would be, uh, Georgia Winters." He put his finger over the mouthpiece. "Mom, the 911 people want to know what's wrong."

"Tell them she's dead."

2

Sirens wailed nearby, making my ears ring and my nerves twitch. Help was arriving quickly, because the fire department was just down the road from the high school. The 911 dispatcher told Tommy and me to stay put, so after I'd done a visual sweep of the room, I sat on a chair next to Marvin's desk in the front of the band room, biting one of my fingernails. Tommy slouched against the wall, hands in his pockets, and stared at the floor.

Despite my best efforts, my gaze kept wandering to the spot where Georgia lay.

Six months ago I had found the stabbed body of Jim Bob Jenkins in the milk case of the local supermarket. That image was forever imprinted in my mind, and I'd only lately reached the point that memories of his lifeless body didn't crop up at weird times. And while I love solving mysteries, death disturbed me, no matter whose it was.

I always wondered if the deceased was ready to meet God.

I deliberately turned my gaze to Tommy. "We need to call and let your father know what's going on." I wasn't sure I wanted to talk to Max right now. He hadn't reacted well to Jim Bob's murder and the ensuing investigation. I wanted to get ahold of my own emotions before I talked to him. I clasped my hands together. "Would you mind calling him?"

I closed my eyes to breathe a quick prayer as Tommy reached for his cell, but we were both interrupted by the entrance of Carla Bickford who stood, hands planted on her hips, glaring at me. "What's happening here? Someone told me an ambulance is on its way. Why didn't you call me first?"

"I was a little distracted." I pointed in the general direction of the body. "Georgia Winters is dead behind the door."

Carla whirled around and stared at Georgia, standing motionless, as if she'd been cast in plaster.

The sirens stopped their hideous shrieks. Moments later paramedics rushed into the room. They ordered Carla out of the way. She exploded to life and walked purposefully from the room, calling Marvin Slade's name.

I wondered where Marvin had been all this time. Music and instrument catalogs covered the surface of his desk, along with a travel mug, two Styrofoam coffee cups, and some other papers. I scooted my chair closer so I could study what was there without disturbing anything.

As the sound of different sirens, probably police, pierced the air, I glimpsed what looked like a receipt sticking out from under a grade book. The top bore the name of a business, but I could only partially read "op" at the end of the name. A distinctive fleur-de-lis decorated the top corner of the paper. I was about to reach over and pull the receipt out to look more closely when two deputies rushed into the room. One made a beeline for Georgia. The other stared at me.

"Are you the one who found her?" he asked, body tense.

"Yes."

"Did you touch anything?"

"Um, well, we probably moved her when we pushed the door open." I wondered if we were in big trouble.

"Who's —"

Someone began barking orders from the hallway, and the deputy raised his hand. "Just a moment, ma'am."

A familiar male voice inquired, "Who was first at the scene?"

Both deputies turned toward the doorway as if yanked by invisible leashes. Detective Eric Scott walked into the band room. I couldn't imagine how he'd gotten here so quickly from the sheriff's office.

The three men spoke briefly, in hushed tones, one deputy motioning toward the body. The other must have said something about me, because Detective Scott's gaze sliced the room until it met mine.

He turned back to the deputies and pointed at a door behind me that led to the instrument storage room. "There's another entrance we can use in the storage area. I've been informed it's kept locked. Get access to that. Work with Fletcher. Make a perimeter, and make sure nobody leaves. Set up places to interview people."

"Yes, sir," they both replied and left the room.

"You." The tall, blond detective motioned at me. "Don't move. Wait for Fletcher." Then he motioned at Tommy. "Go out into the hall and wait." He turned and watched the paramedics.

I didn't bother to say anything. It would do no good. The detective and I were well acquainted from close contact during the investigation into Jim Bob's murder. I knew he could be unbearably bossy when he had a mind to be, especially when I was involved in his investigation.

One of the paramedics turned to him. "She's dead, sir."

I could have told them that. But had she been murdered? And if so, was the weapon the bassoon? I had seen no blood on the instrument, but that didn't mean anything. I hadn't examined it, fearful of messing up evidence.

The sudden sound of yelling filtered through the door from the storage room, and Carla burst back into the room with a deputy on her heels.

Detective Scott whirled around.

"Sorry, sir," the deputy said. "She unlocked the door and ran right past us." He tried to grab her arm.

She evaded his grasp and marched across the room. "Detective."

"Stop right there." His irritation was obvious in his scowl.

She obeyed, but her lips were pursed in displeasure. "I want to know what is going on."

"You need to leave the room right now," he said. "Talk to my corporal."

As if on cue, Corporal Fletcher strode into

24

the room. Both he and the deputy stood behind Carla. Corporal Fletcher's Santa Claus–like appearance probably fooled some people into thinking he was a jovial softie. That impression would be a mistake.

"This is my school," Carla snapped, totally ignoring the corporal. "You know that. And that woman was one of my employees. She was also my friend. . . ." Her voice broke then she took a deep breath and grew angry again. "I have a right to know what's happening. Was this an accident?"

"You need to leave like everyone else," Detective Scott said, ignoring her question and her emotions.

I leaned forward, watching the exchange with interest. If anyone could halt a seemingly unstoppable principal, Detective Scott could. Unfortunately, there's nothing I like better than a good fight, a remnant from my past and something I constantly remind the Lord is not appropriate for a churchgoing mommy. As if He didn't know that already.

"I insist on staying here until I get some answers," she said. "The school board will want a full report. I have a right to know."

Detective Scott's stiff spine was body language I understood. "You'll leave the room on your own or with our help. I don't care. But you'll leave the room."

I had experienced the detective's cold civility, but I'd never heard him on the verge of losing his temper.

Carla squared her shoulders more, which I wouldn't have thought physically possible and stood nose to nose with Detective Scott. "I'm the principal."

"And I'm the detective in charge of this scene." He nodded almost imperceptibly at Corporal Fletcher and the deputy, who closed in on either side of her.

She finally deigned to glance at them and crossed her arms, as if daring them to touch her.

This was more fun than watching parents squabble with referees at the high school football games.

Detective Scott sucked in a deep breath. "I understand you're the principal and you're concerned about your school. I'm sorry, but it's sheriff's office procedure to clear everyone from a scene like this. I assure you that I'll keep you notified of everything you need to know."

A couple seconds ticked by; then Carla heaved a sigh. No doubt she realized she was in the presence of someone whose word and will were backed by his badge and the authority given to him by the sheriff's office. I was impressed. He'd caught his temper before he lost it, but he'd still won. Impressive. That took skill. What Carla probably didn't understand was that "need to know" meant she'd find out very little. Experience had taught me how the detective worked.

I couldn't blame her for listening and obeying. The detective appeared totally intimidating, even to me. Most of the time he wore a suit, but today he had on his uniform, and his black belt bristled with attachments — a telephone, a gun in a holster, and other dangerous looking things I didn't recognize, although I was sure he had handcuffs somewhere.

Before she left the room, Carla pointed at me. "What about *her?*"

Oh, now *that* was mature.

Detective Scott glanced from me to Carla and back again. "I'm questioning *her.*" Then he looked at the corporal. "Fletcher. Interviews. Trish first."

"Yes, sir," Fletcher replied.

By the time Carla had walked out of the room, head held high, Detective Scott was standing over the body. I didn't notice Corporal Fletcher was back in the room until he appeared at my elbow.

"Mrs. C.?" He called me by my nickname

as he waggled his finger at me, indicating I should follow him. I snatched up my purse and obeyed.

Members of the crime scene unit arrived as I left the room. Detective Scott greeted them. I heard him say, "The medical examiner is on the way. I want to know time of death. I don't think it's been long."

We walked through the storage room and into the hallway. There several deputies were herding people around. I caught a glimpse of Tommy, as well as Marvin Slade, whose deep-set, dark eyes looked like black marbles in his narrow, blanched face. If a person ever lived up to the platitude "He looked like he'd seen a ghost," it was Marvin.

Corporal Fletcher led me up the hallway, away from everyone, then pulled out a notebook.

"We didn't move the body on purpose, and I have a good reason to be here," I said before he could ask me anything. I crossed my arms. "It's because of the school play. I'm on the committee. I'm helping with the advertising for the play program. We were supposed to have a meeting today. They're doing *Arsenic and Old Lace.* You know the one. About Mortimer Brewster who finds out his aunts kill off their boarders. Tommy's in the play and . . ." I paused for a breath.

"It's okay, Mrs. C. Just relax." The expression in Corporal Fletcher's eyes was kind under his bushy eyebrows.

"How did you guys get here so fast, anyway?" I asked.

"Sarge and I were on our way here for a meeting with the principal," he said. "The parents are pushing to up the security at the school, and the school board wanted her to talk to law enforcement. The sheriff sent us since Sarge's daughter attends this school."

"Well, they should be concerned — if Georgia was murdered." My thoughts raced. "Do you think she was? Like bashed in the head with the bassoon?"

"We don't know anything right now." He pulled a pen from his pocket. "Just tell me who you were going to meet with."

I dropped my arms to my side. "I was supposed to be meeting with Carla, Marvin Slade, the band director, Connie Gilbert, and . . . Georgia, and a few other people."

"So no one was here when you found the victim except for you and Tommy?" he asked.

"Right. The meeting had been canceled."

"And why was the meeting canceled?"

While I told him, I leaned against the wall to support my suddenly shaky legs. I guessed it was a delayed reaction to finding Georgia. He frowned. "Let's get you somewhere to sit down." He tucked his notebook and pen into his pocket. "Wait here."

As he walked away, I noticed that the crowd in the hallway was considerably smaller. Carla had disappeared. Marvin was gone, too. One deputy was talking to a football player and Kent Smith, the football coach. Kent reminded me of one of my father's favorite bulls, a short and stocky animal with a massive chest and head.

Tommy's face was dark with an emotion I couldn't identify. Maybe fear, which I didn't understand. I wanted to go hug him, but I knew that wouldn't be cool. When I finally caught his gaze, I tried to reassure him with a smile, but he didn't return the gesture. He just looked away and stared at the floor. That disturbed me more than anything else. Tommy had always been the steadiest of our children. No problems at all, unlike his siblings.

I was distracted by a tall teenage girl rushing down the hall past me. Her face looked familiar, but I couldn't place it at the moment. Tommy's expression softened into a smile as she approached. When she stopped in front of him, he bent his head to talk to her in quiet tones.

Uh-oh. I recognized the look. Tommy was smitten.

A few minutes later, a deputy appeared to direct me to the school library. As I walked into the room, I saw Corporal Fletcher attempting to clear the library of the one person who hadn't run down the hall to gawk at the band room door. If the clam-faced librarian ever had a curious bone in her body, she'd shelved it in the reference room's prehistoric section. I had to look closely to make sure she wasn't the mummy of the same librarian who had manned the desk when I attended high school here.

She sniffed and looked askance at the corporal's uniform and gun. "I told the other police officer that I don't think the library is an appropriate place for a police investigation. *Someone* needs to man the front desk."

Corporal Fletcher shrugged and smiled at her as she stood, hands on her hips, glaring at him. "Sorry, ma'am. We're appropriating the library for sheriff's office use with the permission of the principal. You're going to have to leave."

The librarian swiped a stack of books off

the desk and held them to her bosom defensively. "This library is the place where our students come to study. We shouldn't have to close the doors. This is absolutely the last straw. There have been far too many others in here today disturbing our peace. Arguing. Now we have you *police officers.*"

His eyes sharpened with interest. "We're deputies. Now, what other people have been in here arguing?"

She sniffed. "People who should know better."

"Who?" The big man balanced on his toes, reminding me of the first time I met him — right after I found Jim Bob Jensen's body.

She frowned. "What people do in a library is protected. I don't have to tell you."

"Uh-huh." The corporal pulled out a note-pad. "What's your name?"

She wouldn't give him her name and adamantly refused to leave the library. It wasn't until he threatened her with arrest that she finally told him who she was. After that, she turned her back to him and grabbed her square, black pocketbook from her office. "I won't be intimidated." She tilted her chin as she walked out from behind the desk in a huff.

"Oh yeah, I got your number," Corporal Fletcher murmured just loud enough for me to hear. "Liberty for all, and no cops." He winked at me, cleared his throat, and followed her to the door. "I'm sorry. You can take up your complaints with my boss, Sergeant Eric Scott. I'm sure he'd love to discuss proper police procedure with you." The irony in his voice made me smile, especially since I knew Detective Scott and his method of dealing with annoying people.

She didn't catch on. "I *will* speak to him. This is highly inappropriate. The unmitigated gall . . ." She snatched at the handle and yanked open the door. "And to think that a crime has occurred here, on school property. That's because we open our doors to you people. I just don't know. . . ." The door closed, effectively shutting her up.

"Fruitcake," Corporal Fletcher mumbled. "Probably reads too many of those commie books by weirdo political professor types. Sergeant'll slice her to bits."

"Yeah. He's good at slicing. I've experienced a bit of that myself." I felt keyed up and crabby. Probably a result of finding Georgia, hunger, and pregnancy hormones, topped off by bad library memories.

The librarian clone who had just walked out was like the one who had banished me from the hallowed book cloister when I was in school. That was because I hit a classmate

33

with a sacred *National Geographic* and inadvertently ripped the cover. When strange things started happening to the librarian, like the day she discovered a formaldehyde-preserved frog in place of the meat in her sandwich, I was briefly expelled. That was the first and last time my daddy ever tanned my hide. But then, my parents never knew half the stuff I did when I was young.

"Say, Mrs. C., don't you worry about Sarge." Corporal Fletcher must have seen the scowl on my face, but he misinterpreted it. "You'll be fine."

I stiffened my shoulders and stared out the window. How long would I be stuck here? "He's not acting real nice today." I was dreading talking to the sergeant, especially since Tommy and I had moved the body.

"Umm . . . yeah, well, probably," the corporal said behind me. "To be expected."

I faced him. "Why?"

From his narrowed eyes, I could tell he was thinking, but I wasn't sure what about. "Well, a possible crime in a school is bad news. Real political. We got a couple of new county commissioners who are being a real pain right now. That and the citizen advisory board. Now this."

"That's no excuse for grumpiness." Even as I said it, I realized it was the proverbial pot calling the kettle black. I wasn't little Miss Sunshine today, myself.

Corporal Fletcher glanced over his shoulder then sidled up closer to me. "You gotta give people leeway, Mrs. C. Things happen. I'm sure you're aware of that. You have good . . . sources. You hear things. Now, why don't you sit down?" He pulled a chair out from under a table.

I opened my mouth to ask what he was talking about, but he avoided my gaze.

"I'm going to get you a bottle of water," he said. "We can't have you fainting or something."

That was sweet of him. He probably recalled the time I sort of fell into his arms after I had been threatened by a murderer.

"I need to call Max."

"You do that. I'll be right back."

I pulled out my cell phone and reluctantly speed-dialed Max's cell. He was overly protective on a good day, but with me being pregnant . . .

I braced myself for a lecture, but Max didn't pick up. Perversely, I felt annoyed with him, and I left a message that probably let him know how I felt.

After I snapped my phone closed, Corporal Fletcher's words ran through my mind. He'd implied that I might know something by way of gossip. Too antsy to sit, I began pacing the library. What did he mean? Had I missed something important?

I was sorely tempted to make notes. During the investigation into Jim Bob's murder, I'd discovered I liked making mystery lists and solving crimes. Afterward, I bought a stack of steno pads, just in case — steno pads being small enough to tuck into my purse but large enough to keep decent notes. My mind began a mental debate. Georgia's death intrigued me as much as it chilled me, and somehow, being that interested didn't seem quite proper.

By the time Corporal Fletcher returned and gave me a bottle of water and package of crackers, intrigue had won over propriety. I was jotting down my thoughts on an old grocery receipt I found in my purse. I told myself that my motives were noble. I knew the detective would want to know in detail what I had observed, so this would be handy.

I hated packaged crackers, but I ate them because Corporal Fletcher had been nice enough to buy them. Besides, they would stave off my hunger pains. He disappeared again, leaving me alone with my thoughts.

As I swallowed the last dry crumbs, Detective Scott burst into the room, followed closely by the corporal. "I'm going to interview Tommy," the detective said when I looked up.

"That's fine."

"Fletcher, send someone to find my daughter. Then get Tommy. The medical examiner said that . . ." His voice trailed off as he glanced at me; then he motioned toward the hallway with his head. Corporal Fletcher followed him out the door. Well, that was a pointed and not very nice way to let me know I wasn't in the loop.

When he walked back into the library, I glanced up. "We didn't move the body on purpose."

"I know that," he said.

"So I'm not in trouble?"

"Not as far as I can tell right now." He yanked a chair from under a table and dragged it in front of me.

Since trouble and Trish are synonymous, that wouldn't last. I stared back down at my list.

"What are you writing?" he asked me irritably.

"Notes." I chewed on the pen.

"I knew it." Detective Scott sat down hard on the chair with an exaggerated sigh.

"Trish."

I looked up at him. "Yes?"

"Why are you making notes?" His expression hadn't changed from earlier in the band room.

"Well, it helps me remember everything, and then I can help you better." Unfortunately, he knew about my mystery lists. Me and my big mouth. I'd told him during the investigation into Jim Bob's murder.

"Listen to me," he said. "I just need your statement. I don't need your help."

"There's a difference?" I asked.

"You know exactly what I mean." His right eye twitched. "I don't want to have to worry about you. Especially now that you're expecting. Last time was plenty for me. I'm sure Max would agree."

"Oh, I get it." I gripped my pen tighter. "You're threatening to tell Max that I was sitting here making notes. And you hope he will keep me under control and make me stop."

"Got it in one." Detective Scott pulled a notebook from his pocket.

His attitude was reminiscent of the way he'd acted in the past. So was my immediate annoyance with him.

"Your reaction must mean that this was a murder," I said.

He eyed me. "We don't know anything yet."

"Right. As usual. And you really won't *know* anything until the case is solved, at which time you'll tell me everything I *need* to know." I looked at my list, fighting a growing sense of irritation.

His breath hissed through his teeth. "Trish, would you please pay attention and answer my questions?"

"Of course." I laid the pen and paper on my knees and folded my hands on my stomach. "I'm listening."

The nerve at the corner of his eye continued to twitch. "Why do I feel like you're just tolerating me?"

I shrugged.

He tapped his pen on his notebook. "Were you alone when you found Georgia?"

"No. Tommy was with me."

He jotted a note. "Did you and Tommy arrive together?"

I frowned. "No, he was already here."

The detective's eyes narrowed, and he bounced his pen on his leg. *Tap, tap, tap.* "Was he with you when you discovered Georgia?"

"Yes . . . well." I met his gaze. "He got to the band room right after I did, but he noticed her first."

"I want to know everything you saw from the moment you pulled into the school parking lot."

I took a deep breath, pointedly picked up my pen, lifted the paper, and shook it for emphasis. I heard him sigh as I began to read. He interrupted me when I mentioned Connie.

"Connie who?" he asked.

"Gilbert. She does the costumes for the play. I spoke to her in Georgia's classroom before I went to the band room."

He made a note. "All right. Proceed."

He didn't interrupt me again, and when I finished, I put the paper down and stared at him.

"Thank you," he said as he jotted down notes. He glanced up at me. "Now, tell me again exactly what you saw when you were walking up to the victim," he said. "You skipped that part."

I swallowed. I didn't want to talk about that. I didn't want to remember Georgia Winters's dead body.

"I'm sorry, Trish," he said in a softer tone. "This is very difficult for you, I know. I can arrange for you to talk to a victim advocate if you'd like."

That made me get ahold of myself. I'd met his victim advocate. She was very sweet, with one of those soft voices pitched just right to be soothing. Anyone who acted like that couldn't possibly be real, and that made me suspicious.

"No, thanks. I'm fine." I told him exactly what I'd seen. "My biggest question is how whoever murdered her — if she was murdered — got out of the band room. There was a chair behind the door to the room, you know."

He asked me to describe that to him again, which I did.

"I didn't even look at the door in the instrument storage room," I said, "but you said it was locked, right?"

"Is that all?" Of course he didn't answer me, just tapped his pen hard on his leg.

"Yes," I said.

"Are you sure?"

"Aren't I always sure?" I slapped the paper on my lap, irritated at him again.

"Unfortunately."

But before I could ask him what, exactly, *that* meant, I heard the library door open. I turned and saw Tommy holding it for the pretty teenage girl he'd been talking to in the hall. Now I remembered where I'd seen her face. From a photo in Detective Scott's office.

"Hey, Daddy," she said. "You remember

41

my car is in the shop?"

Tommy looked at me then at Detective Scott, who wasn't smiling.

"I remember," he said to his daughter.

"Well, Tommy was supposed to drive me home so we could practice a little more. I'll wait until you're done talking to him."

The detective's gaze had fallen on my son, like a scientist studying a germ under a microscope. Finally, he looked back at his daughter. "I'll have one of the deputies drive you home. I'm going to talk to Tommy next. We could be here for a while."

A flash of anger lit her eyes. "I don't want to ride home with one of your people. Can't I just wait for Tommy?"

Detective Scott glanced from her to my stepson, frowning. "Uh, no. I want you to go home. Why don't you call your aunt Elissa?"

The anger remained in his daughter's eyes. "I know what's going on. It's all over the school. Ms. Winters got bashed in the head. A lot of people were mad at her. But Tommy and I still need to practice."

What the detective's daughter had said just dawned on me. "You're in the play, too?"

She and Tommy exchanged chummy grins.

"Yeah, isn't it great?" she said.

"Sherry's got the part of Elaine," Tommy said. "I've got the part of Mortimer Brewster."

I met Detective Scott's startled gaze. For one of the very first times, I could precisely read his thoughts. Dismay. Our teenagers were in the same play. Their parts involved romance. With each other.

3

Detective Scott cleared his throat. Tommy and Sherry severed their glances.

"I'd like to speak with you in the hall," the detective said to his daughter.

She whirled on her heel without a word and headed for the library door. He followed her with a stiff back.

This wasn't good. Neither was Tommy's expression. Worry creased his brow.

"Detective Scott wants to talk to you," I said. "I do, too."

"Yeah," Tommy said. "But I gotta get to work after he talks to me, and I still have to get my algebra book from my locker."

I glanced at my watch. "I'll go get the book and then wait for you. Why don't you give me the combination?"

"Okay, but can't we talk later?" he asked.

Was he avoiding me? "No, I'll wait," I said. "I'll go get the book right now; then I'll be back. We can talk on the way to your car."

Tommy told me how to get into his locker. Then, as I reached for the library door handle, Detective Scott opened the doors and passed me with a frown on his face.

Out in the hall, Sherry stood with her face twisted in a scowl, watching her father shut the doors. She noticed me and made an effort to smile, then turned to leave. She was heading the same way I was.

I stepped up and walked next to her. "I'm going to Tommy's locker to get a book."

"I'm going there, too. My locker is in the same hall. Corporal Fletcher is meeting me." Her words were chopped and tense.

"He's a nice man," I said by way of trying to soothe her.

"Yeah, maybe, but he's my dad's friend."

She said "dad's friend" as if it were a bad word. Things were definitely not good at the Scott household. Maybe I could distract her by asking her some questions.

"So, how long have you and Tommy known each other?" I thought it odd that he hadn't mentioned her before. The school wasn't that large.

"Only this year," she said. "We met the first day of school. He helped me settle in. I was in a private school before." She glanced at me. "I lived with my mom until this year."

"Where was that?" I asked.

45

"Virginia Beach," she said. "My stepdad is in the military. He just got transferred overseas."

"It must be rough to switch schools so close to graduation."

She shrugged. "I'm used to moving around. I wanted to go with them."

"And you couldn't?"

She shook her head, brows lowered. "All the adults got together and made the decision. Nobody asked me what I wanted." The tone of her voice was too bitter for a girl her age.

"Your dad mentioned your aunt. Is that his sister?"

Sherry nodded. "Yeah, Aunt Elissa. She's moved in with me and dad for this year." She glanced at me. "They say it's because she's on leave right now and needs to rethink her life. I know it's because they're worried about me and think someone has to watch out for me."

I glanced at her and realized there was far more to her than met the eye. "Any particular reason they think that?"

She stared straight ahead. "I don't always do what I'm told."

I wondered what, exactly, that meant. She didn't look like she used drugs, but one couldn't always tell by physical appearance.

She peeked at me and read my thoughts correctly. "It's nothing like you're thinking. I just have definite ideas about how things should be. I didn't want to move in with my dad, and I threatened to run away."

That made me smile. "I threatened to run away a lot when I was in high school."

"You did?" She seemed surprised.

"Sure."

"Well, what did your parents do?"

"My mother offered to help me pack."

Sherry stared at me in disbelief; then she laughed, a contagious sound that made me join in. "Wow. That's reverse psychology, isn't it?"

"Yeah, but it turned out okay. Nobody got that upset, which really helped calm me down."

"I wish my dad was calm." The expression on her face became gloomy.

"He's worried, I'm sure. If you haven't lived with him before this, he's probably feeling overwhelmed."

"Yeah, that's what Aunt Elissa says."

By that time, we'd reached the hall where the lockers were located. I stopped short. I saw Corporal Fletcher and another deputy poking around in a locker, while a third looked on.

I charged up to them. "What are you doing? Is that Tommy's?"

"No need to get excited, Mrs. C.," the corporal said. "We're just doing a routine investigation."

"Yes, but why Tommy's locker?" I wondered if this had to do with Detective Scott questioning him. Was my son a suspect?

The corporal gently took my elbow. I allowed him to pull me away, mostly because I knew I wouldn't have any choice in the matter. Sherry's cold and distant expression as she watched the other deputy work reminded me of her father.

When the corporal and I had walked a ways down the hall, he let go of my arm. "Everything is fine. We just need to eliminate Tommy."

"Eliminate him? From what? Is he . . ." My voice trailed off. Tommy had been in the right place at the right time to commit murder. This was not good. Not at all.

I got back to the library just in time for Tommy to open the door.

"I have to get to work," he said.

"I know. I'll walk with you to your car."

"Did you get my algebra book?" he asked.

"Yes." I glanced at him. "*After* I convinced the deputies searching your locker to give it to me."

Tommy's nostrils flared. "They were searching my locker? Why?"

"To eliminate you," I said.

He took a deep breath. "I just talked to Dad."

"You reached him?"

"Yeah. I caught him just when he was leaving a meeting."

"And?" I asked.

"I told him everything is fine. He was really worried about you, but I told him that you're okay. He told me to tell you to call him when you get home. He'll keep his phone on vibrate, so even if he's in a meeting, he can get it."

I felt like Tommy was trying to distract me, so I gave him my mother eye. "Is everything really fine?"

"Yes."

The mother eye didn't work. He wouldn't look at me. "What did Detective Scott ask you?"

Tommy stared straight ahead. "Probably the same things he asked you."

"And that would be?"

"Just why I was here and what I was doing. I told him I was practicing."

We reached the door that led to the parking lot. "So, what's with you and Sherry?"

He shrugged. "She's really cool. We're in

the play together."

I suspected she was more than cool, but he wasn't going to tell me. Besides, his legs were so long, and he was walking so fast, I was having trouble keeping up with him.

"Someone told me you were looking for Georgia?"

We'd reached his car, and he unlocked the door. "Yeah, I had to talk to her. Listen, I have to get to work." He leaned down and kissed my forehead, an action so like his father that I couldn't speak. "It'll all be okay; you just wait and see."

I considered Tommy's words as I stopped by the local Dairy Delite for a chocolate milk shake. I needed something in my stomach besides packaged crackers. My nerves felt ragged, like they'd been scraped raw on a cement sidewalk. I hoped that something sweet and chocolaty would soothe me.

When a picture of Georgia's body flickered through my mind, I deliberately turned my thoughts to other things. The problem was, everything that came to mind right now was disturbing. I wasn't well enough acquainted with Georgia to know whether she had known the Lord. And then there was Tommy. The fact that he'd made so much effort to assure me not to worry made me worried. What was so significant that Detective Scott had reason to search Tommy's locker? How big a suspect was he?

As I pulled around to the drive-through, I finally hit on a good memory. All the nights I'd come here with my best friend, Abbie, when we were in high school. That made me realize I hadn't spoken to her in a couple of days. I really needed to talk to her now.

At the drive-up window, I looked inside and saw the manager. I waved at her out of politeness, and she hustled over to the window, pushing aside the teenager who had just taken my order.

"Trish! Oh my! I heard about what happened at the school. How horrible for you!"

"It wasn't pleasant." She had a habit of speaking in exclamation points.

She leaned out the window, her chest smashed on the sill. I wondered if it hurt.

"I can just imagine!" She tried to wiggle closer to me, and I was afraid she was going to cut herself in half. "What was it like?"

"What was what like?" I asked.

"You know," she said in a stage whisper. She glanced over her shoulder, which put her at risk for losing her balance and falling out the window. "Finding her. I can't even imagine that."

"Um . . . it was unpleasant?" Her relish for details about Georgia's death was going to ruin my appetite for a milk shake.

She nodded as though I'd said something terribly profound. "I understand, I really do."

I doubted that. Not unless she'd ever found a dead body.

"You know," she said. "She was the kind of person who was easy to be mad at."

Her comment rang a bell, and I remembered that Sherry Scott had said something similar.

"How come?" I asked.

"Oh! I went to school with her, you know. She was overbearing, but lately!"

"Lately?" I asked.

"Well, she's gotten a real attitude. Especially with her family. I'm sure there are a few people who will be happy she's dead."

Happy? What a dreadful thing to say. Someone called her name at the same time my milk shake arrived. I watched with relief as she pulled herself back inside the window.

As I drove away, I passed the strip mall where my mother had her doughnut shop, Doris's Doughnuts. I thought about stopping, but I didn't want to face the grilling I'd get there. I'd wait until I got home to call her.

The milk shake had the desired effect. In just a few miles, my stomach wasn't churning anymore. I had managed to tamp down all my screaming worries and enjoy the scenery. Only two minutes out of town in any direction and everything turns to farm fields. I could tell fall was coming. The lush fields were no longer green with growth. The trees would start changing colors soon.

The serene landscape made me feel peaceful. I took a deep breath, relaxed my shoulders, and began to look forward to my evening with Max. When my cell phone rang again, I eagerly dug it out of my purse, but when I glanced at the little screen, my heart plummeted. It was my mother.

4

I debated answering my cell phone at all. I love my mother, but I don't always like talking to her. That's because of the conversational arrows I have to evade. Still, she'd probably heard about the murder, and I didn't want her to worry.

I pushed the button and jammed the phone against my ear. "Hi, Ma. Did Daddy pick up Charlie and Sammie after school?"

"Of course he did," she said. "When we say we'll babysit, we always do it. We don't ignore things like some people do. I saw you drive right by the shop. I can't believe you didn't stop, and you haven't called me. Once again, I'm the last to know that my daughter is involved in a crime."

I sighed. "I'm not involved in a crime. I don't even know if it really *was* a crime. Maybe it was an accident. Besides, I haven't even talked to Max yet, so you aren't left out."

"Well, I'm your mother. And it was a crime. I heard it was murder. I nearly had a heart attack. One day you're going to kill me. It's just hard to believe that I actually carried you for nine months and you could be so insensitive. And the labor was the worst pain of my life. . . ."

I tuned her out and stared at the road ahead of me while she finished telling me in detail the agony she went through to have me and why I should feel guilty. I'd heard it all so many times I could have lectured myself.

". . . as if your ignoring me isn't enough, I also heard that someone is planning to bring a large housing development into Four Oaks. Can you imagine that? I mean —"

I nearly ran off the road. "What?"

"I knew you weren't listening to me." She clucked her tongue.

I hoped I wasn't in for another lengthy discourse about how grateful I should be that I was born before she explained what she'd just said. To my relief, she was eager to share the little she knew.

"I found out today at the shop that someone is planning to bring a housing development to our town."

Doris's Doughnuts was the source of anything newsworthy in Four Oaks and the surrounding vicinity. Well, *newsworthy* was a misnomer. *Gossip* was a better word. Still, chances were that anything coming from my mother had at least a grain of truth in it. I was horrified.

"Can you imagine?" she asked. "After housing developments come shopping centers. Big ones. With hardware stores and fast-food places and . . . doughnut shops." Her voice cracked, and I felt bad for her. She'd worked hard to build up her business.

I doubted anyone could really compete with my mother, but I wouldn't bother to try to assure her. She'd just argue. "So you don't know anything else? Like who would think of doing such a thing?" An influx of new people and the traffic and noise would destroy everything I loved about country living. Slowly the countryside would be eaten up by "progress."

"We've seen it happening in counties closer to the city," Ma said. "Why, the next thing you know, we could be the gambling capital of the East Coast. Look at what they tried to do in Gettysburg. A casino and slot machines. What were they thinking? Why, I wouldn't be a bit surprised if Georgia Winters was killed by some mob stranger coming in and scouting out the land."

I tried to picture guys in black suits crawling around Four Oaks looking for people to murder. "Come on, Ma. That's a little bit dramatic."

"You think so? April said that Georgia wanted to sell off her granny's farm, and there you go. She lived there, you know. The perfect place for a casino. It's all about commerce. Greed. Avarice."

Avarice? My mother was developing quite a vocabulary, even if her word choices were redundant.

"What purpose would be served by the mob killing Georgia?"

"Why, to get the farm, of course."

"Oh." I wasn't going to pursue it further right now. I'd reached my house, which is in a very small rural development. The only one in Four Oaks and the only one I wanted to see here — ever. I pulled into the driveway and punched the button on the garage door opener. "Well, we'll see, I guess."

"You mark my words," my mother said. "It's all about greediness. Selfishness."

"Okay. Well, I'm home now. I need to go. I have to call Max."

"Well, I hope you learned a lesson. I mean —"

"I did," I agreed, even though I wasn't exactly sure what lesson I was supposed to have learned except not to answer my cell phone when my mother called.

"Well, good."

"I'll talk to you later. Tell Daddy hello."

"This will just kill him," she said.

Whatever "this" was. And I doubted that anything would shake him up. My daddy was an unflappable kind of guy. He had to be to live with my mother. I hung up and then dialed Max as I pulled into the garage. I hoped he was already on his way home. I could get things ready quickly.

"Trish?" He answered on the third ring. "Baby, I'm so glad to hear from you. Are you okay?"

"Yeah." His use of my favorite pet name always made me a little weak in the knees. A dangerous thing for someone in my condition. "How are you?" I got out of the SUV and went inside.

"Hectic," he said. "Worried about you. Tommy told me everything. I'm sorry I couldn't get the phone when you called. I was stuck in meetings."

"I'm fine. Really." In the kitchen, I tossed my purse on the table.

He sighed. "I can't say I'm surprised this happened."

My poor husband. He says living with me is like riding a roller coaster. He never knows what to expect next.

"Well, at least I didn't sprain or break anything." In the past, my habit of joining my kids in activities like Rollerblading had landed me in the hospital more than once.

He inhaled. "Don't even say that. You've managed to stay out of the hospital for almost nine months. The next time you go there, I want it to be when the baby is born."

"That shouldn't be a problem," I said. "I'm being really good. Are you on your way home?"

"Not yet."

Well, that gave me a little more time to take a bath and put on my dress.

"So, Tommy told you everything, right?" I wondered if he'd told his father that Detective Scott had questioned him like a suspect.

"Everything?" Max asked quickly. "Like what?"

"Well, about us finding Georgia and all," I said.

"Yes. Well, he said you two found Georgia behind the door. That must have been pretty traumatic for you. Are you sure you're all right?"

"Yes, although it was a little bloodier than when I found Jim Bob." I thought I heard Max groan. "Then Detective Scott questioned us. Both of us. Separately."

"And a lot of other people," Max said. "Tommy said just about everyone was pulled aside."

"So that's not unusual?" I asked.

"Not at all. You should remember that from last time you were . . . uh, involved in a murder."

"I wasn't *involved.* I just found the body."

"Isn't finding the body being involved?" he asked.

"Well, not like that. Like I committed a crime or something. But, whatever. This time was different . . . there were just more of us, including Tommy." I opened the refrigerator to take out the steaks so I could marinate them.

"Well, he found the body with you. I wouldn't expect anything different."

Perhaps I was overreacting to Detective Scott's attitude. Maybe he was just a protective father who wasn't thrilled about his daughter liking a boy, and that's what accounted for the hard looks he gave Tommy.

"When will you be home?" I asked. "I'm just about to start dinner."

His pause was long enough to tell me he wasn't sure. "I've got one more meeting." He paused again. "I don't want to be insensitive. You said you're okay, but you've been through a lot today. I could leave if you need me to."

I slammed the refrigerator door shut on the steaks. As usual, he was being fair, but I could read between the lines. This meeting was important. Besides, I'd already told him I was fine. I couldn't reverse myself and be traumatized. Yes, I wanted him to come home right now, but I didn't "need" him to.

I decided to try a different tact. Whining. "The meeting is that important?"

"Yes, otherwise I would be home already. I worry about you."

I felt guilty for making him feel bad, but that didn't stop me from continuing. "Well, I had a nice dinner planned —"

"Do you think it can wait until tomorrow?" he asked. "Maybe you and the kids can go out."

"The kids are with my mother," I said. "And speaking of my mother, she told me that someone is planning to build a huge housing development in Four Oaks."

Through the receiver, I heard voices in the background. "Hang on a second," Max said.

I waited and felt sorry for myself. Not only had I found a dead woman, but Four Oaks was threatened with a housing development. And to top it off, I wanted time alone with my husband, but —

"Trish?"

"Is the meeting canceled?" I could always hope.

"Uh, no. In fact, I need to go right now. Are you sure you're okay?"

I sighed. "Yes, I guess so."

"I'm sorry. Thank you for understanding."

"You're welcome," I murmured.

"I'll be home as soon as possible. I love you."

"I love you, too." I put the phone down and rested my chin in my hand.

The last month or so, Max seemed to be drifting away from me, spending more time at work and less time at home. Granted, we'd been married for almost seven years, but up until now, the romantic part of our marriage was perfect. At least as perfect as it could be with so many kids around and my pregnancy, which, I reminded myself, was a miracle. I'd been told I couldn't have any more children.

But miracle pregnancy or not, this one was tougher on me than when I was carrying Sammie. I had pains where I hadn't had pains before, and I fought exhaustion daily.

I shifted on the hard chair and glanced around my yellow and white kitchen. I needed a distraction from my self-pity, which was stupid and selfish. Things could be worse. Much worse. At least I was alive, unlike poor Georgia. She'd never have the opportunity to feel sorry for herself again.

Why would somebody kill her? What could a high school English teacher have done to bring out that kind of passion in someone? What motive could somebody possibly have to murder her?

I was becoming curious. And Detective Scott's insistence that I not get involved egged me on. One of my biggest faults was wanting to do the things I shouldn't do. Maybe I was a bit like Sherry that way.

I glanced at the drawer where I'd stored the steno pads I'd bought months ago; then my gaze slid up to the counter above the drawer, where I'd left my Bible and the booklet from my women's Bible study. That's what I *should* be doing. We were studying the fruit of the Spirit: love, joy, peace, patience, kindness, goodness, faithfulness, gentleness, and self-control. Definitely a Bible study I needed.

I walked to the counter and glanced at the Bible study. This week's lesson was on love. The first item of discussion was *Love is action, not always feeling.* I bit a fingernail in indecision. Bible study or clue notebook? I decided I was too keyed up to study. I'd feel better after I wrote down all my clues.

I whispered a quick "I'm sorry" to the Lord, yanked a steno pad from the drawer, and picked up my Bible study booklet. I returned to the table where I dug in my purse and pulled out a pen and the receipt on which I'd written my clues earlier. Then I stuffed the booklet into my purse. I'd read through it at work tomorrow.

I opened the notebook to the first blank page and bit the end of my pen. Although Georgia's death could have been an accident, I doubted it. Not the way Detective Scott had spoken about the medical examiner to Corporal Fletcher.

From previous experience, I knew that clues are only as good as a sleuth's observations. Things that didn't seem important at first could gain great significance later. With that in mind, I set my pen to paper.

Section I. The Scene: Georgia dead in the band room behind the door. Wound on her head. Bassoon lying on the floor near her. Chairs knocked over. Music on the floor.

Who should be on my initial suspect list? Realistically, every person at the school at the time Georgia was killed — which was the reason Detective Scott had to follow up on everyone, including my son.

One thing I knew from past experience

was that everything hinged around the victim.

On the same page I wrote, *The Victim: Georgia Winters.*

What had I heard about her today? *Developed an attitude lately with her family. Lives with her granny. Might want to sell off the farm.*

And when, exactly, *was* she killed? I wasn't sure about that, but I figured from what the detective said to the crime scene people that she hadn't been dead long when we found her.

I thought about my mother's comment. What were the chances of a stranger breaking into the school and killing Georgia over a potential housing development? Slim to none. But what about a stranger breaking in period? Although I hated to think about it, crimes in schools were on the rise.

I went to page two. *Section II. Questions/ Observations: 1. Was Georgia murdered? 2. If so, how? Was it the bassoon? 3. How did the murderer get out of the room? Through the door in the storage room?* I needed to get a look at that.

I flipped over five pages to leave room for more questions and wrote, *Section III. Suspects:* Who had been there at the time? *Marvin Slade. Carla Bickford. Connie Gilbert.*

Who else?

Coach Kent Smith. Football players. Other teachers? Students? I could rule out Tommy, but what about his classmates? Would any of them have a reason to kill Georgia?

Perhaps it had been someone who didn't work at the school or attend but had known her. *One of Georgia's acquaintances. Who?* Then I wrote, *A complete stranger.*

I jotted notes about where I thought people had been. Had Connie still been at the school when I found Georgia's body or had she left after I had spoken with her?

I was going to have to do some snooping around the school. That would be difficult because I had no good reason to be there except for play committee meetings. I wondered if Carla would cancel our next meeting due to Georgia's murder. I doubted it. Her credo was probably "The show must go on."

I flipped back to Section II and added a couple more things. *Carla and Georgia were supposed to go out to dinner. Were they friends?*

My stomach growled. The milk shake hadn't lasted long. I laid the pen on the notebook and noticed for the first time since I'd arrived how lifeless the house felt. Sammie and Charlie were still at my folks' house. Tommy and Karen were both working.

I should do something productive like finish sewing the curtains for the baby's room. In a frenzy of homemaking insanity, I'd decided to make everything myself. Thus, patterns and fabric littered a corner of the family room where I kept my sewing machine. I needed to get everything done, but . . . better yet, I could put it off and go see Abbie.

I dialed her number. The phone rang six times; then her machine picked up.

I jiggled my foot in frustration. As soon as the message ended, I began yammering. "Abbie, where are you? I need you. I want to talk. Please call —"

I heard a click. "Trish?" Abbie breathed into the receiver. "Sorry."

"Are you monitoring your calls?"

"Sort of. I heard about Georgia. I was going to call you shortly. Are you okay?"

"I'm okay, but I need company," I said. "I'm alone."

"Where is everyone?" Abbie didn't really understand how I felt about an empty house. I'm social to the extreme. She loves her solitary life, writing her suspense novels in her store-top apartment.

"My oldest are out doing their normal activities. The youngest ones are at my folks' house. And Max is working late. Again."

"I'm sorry," she repeated. "You know what? I could really use a break. How about I come over and help you work on the nursery?"

"I don't feel like sewing," I said. "I was at the Dairy Delite today and remembered how we used to cruise. It made me miss you and want to go out."

"Oh wow." She laughed. "To be that young again . . . or maybe not. Anyway, that sounds perfect. I'm starving. Yes. Why don't we go to that little Mexican place over in Plummerville? I'll pick you up in, say, thirty minutes?"

By the time Abbie pulled in my driveway, I'd changed into maternity jeans and an orange stretchy shirt — a normal one. I looked like a basketball tummy. I didn't care. I was tired of wearing baggy shirts that pretended to cover everything but only made me look like a cloth-draped pear with legs. The pants felt snug, but they'd just come out of the dryer. Besides, my stomach was getting huge.

At the last minute, I snatched my steno clue notebook from the table and stuffed it into my purse.

Abbie pecked my cheek with a light kiss after I'd crawled into her red Mustang. I loved her car. A convertible. Sometimes in the summer, we'd put the top down and go out cruising like we had when we were teenagers. Only back then, we used an old pickup truck.

"So talk to me."

She always says that. And I always oblige. I proceeded to whine about Max working late when I'd planned a romantic dinner. I was in the middle of telling her about the black dress I'd bought to entice him when she interrupted me.

"Did you tell him ahead of time about your plans?"

I stuck my chin in the air. "Well, no, Miss I'm-on-Max's-Side. I wanted to surprise him."

She smiled. "How could you expect him to know what you were thinking?"

She sounded so reasonable and logical. I didn't want to be reasonable or logical, so I just crossed my arms and frowned at her. "He should come home at night."

She laughed softly. "You know he adores you. Maybe he's just got a lot going on right now."

"You're my best friend," I said. "You're supposed to be on my side. You've always been on my side."

"Okay, okay." She turned a corner, moving the car smoothly from gear to gear. "He's a beast. He treats you horribly, and you're absolutely miserable."

I slapped her arm. "Use sarcasm on me. You're right, of course."

When we reached the restaurant, we got a corner booth. Colorful piñatas hung from the ceiling. Brightly painted panoramas embellished tan plaster walls. Recorded mariachi music blasted from the speakers. We ordered then settled back with chips and salsa. I finally noticed that Abbie didn't look so good. Sort of tense, with lines on her forehead and around her eyes, like she had a headache.

"You okay?" I asked.

"Mostly." She took a sip of iced tea and didn't look at me.

"Are you sure?"

She put down her glass. "Why don't we talk about you? That's why we're here."

She wasn't acting right at all, but Abbie was a private person even with me, and we'd known each other since kindergarten. Sometimes I had to work to get her to open up. In that regard, she was a bit like her grandmother, the woman who had raised her. Although Abbie wasn't the repressive, overly religious person her grandmother had been, she had some of the same personality traits. I'd wait a few minutes and try again.

"So," Abbie met my gaze, "you want to tell me about Georgia?"

I took a deep breath. "Not gory details, really, because it's kind of icky. Especially when we're about to eat."

"We can talk about something else if you want to."

"No. It's fine. I need to talk about it." I took a deep breath and explained how I'd arrived at the band room and when Tommy showed up.

Abbie was shaking her head.

"What?" I asked.

"I know it's horrible, but still . . . bashed in the head in the band room. Only you could find someone in a situation like that. Are you going to play sleuth?"

I must have blushed, because Abbie smiled. "You can't help it, can you? You're terribly curious."

"Well, there is that, but I'm also a little bit worried. I'm pretty sure she was murdered."

"Was there any doubt?" Abbie asked.

I shrugged. "You know how noncommittal the cops are. I guess it could have been an accident. She could have fallen and hit her head, but some things in the room were wrecked. Like there'd been a struggle."

"Sounds like a fight to me," Abbie said. "Why are you worried?"

"Tommy was questioned."

She raised her eyebrows. "Really?"

"Yes, but I can't imagine why except that he was there with me. What possible motive could he have?" I went on to tell her all the other people I considered possible suspects.

Abbie nodded. "You know that Georgia moved in with her granny Nettie two years ago? Nettie isn't doing well."

"Really?" I fumbled in my purse for my notebook. "Nettie Winters? How do you know that?"

"Nettie was quite a gardener. Remember? That's where I used to get my cut flowers and herbs."

"Yes, now that you mention it. What's wrong with her?"

"Not sure, but her health is failing." Abbie frowned. "So you *are* going to play sleuth?"

I shrugged. "Maybe. Maybe not. But Mr. Bossy Police Person Detective Eric Scott told me to mind my own business. I hate it when he does that."

Abbie picked up a chip and jabbed it in the salsa.

"He was in a horrible mood. He practically yelled at Carla; not that she didn't

deserve it, but usually he's cooler than that."
I took a swig of water. "You know what was really weird? Corporal Fletcher implied something odd was going on."

Abbie chewed her chip hard.

"You know Detective Scott's daughter is living with him now. I met her today. She's not a happy camper. I wonder why he never got married again." I stuffed a salsa-laden chip into my mouth then attempted to speak through it. "It's really no wonder. He's personality challenged."

Our server arrived with our food. Abbie and I asked the Lord to bless the food; then I dug into my taco salad with gusto, in spite of knowing that even if it was blessed, I'd pay later with acid reflux. We ate in silence for a few minutes; then I noticed Abbie was just pushing her tacos around her plate.

"Are you okay, Abs?" I asked. "You're not sick, are you? You don't look so hot. The way you're acting, you'd think that you had a run-in with Detective Scott, too."

Abbie's fork hit the plate.

That got my attention. "Did you? Did he give you a ticket or something?"

"I wish it was that." Her lips were pursed.

I put my fork down. "Stop doing that with your mouth. You look like your grandmother, and that gives me the creeps."

She tried to relax her lips but didn't succeed.

"Abs, he didn't arrest you for something, did he? You go to all lengths to research your books, but you didn't do anything wrong, did you? Just for your books? I mean, that would be kind of funny if you didn't get a record because of it."

She coughed and shook her head.

"Well then, what?"

She took a deep breath but avoided my eyes. "He asked me out."

5

I felt stupid. Why hadn't I seen this coming? During the investigation into Jim Bob's murder, I'd noticed Detective Scott watching Abbie with appreciation. Of course, with her long red hair and legs that go on forever, most guys watched her that way. I'd be jealous if I didn't love her. Still, if I hadn't been intuitive enough to see this, how in the world did I think I could solve a crime?

I reached across the table and touched her hand. "Are you going?"

She finally met my eyes. "No."

I pushed my plate away. "I think it's time you talk to me."

"I don't want to talk about it."

"I'm not going to let this slide, so you might as well give it up."

She glared at me. "Fine. Then you might as well know."

I leaned back and waited while she picked at the food on her plate.

"You know somebody at the sheriff's office fobbed me off on Eric a year and a half ago, right?"

"You mean to ask writing questions? Like a consultant? That wasn't your idea?"

She shook her head. "No, it wasn't. My old consultant retired. I have no idea why I ended up with Eric, but I did. My old consultant just kept telling me to go with the flow. Eric had the experience I needed for my books. Things have been okay. I only talk to him when it's necessary." She looked away from me. "This time, I was sitting in his office with a list of questions, but he wasn't really paying much attention, which frustrated me. Finally, I asked him if I should come back at a better time. He bounced his pen a few times and then asked me out."

I knew Detective Scott's pen bouncing routine. It meant he was either thinking or disturbed. "So you turned him down?"

"I was so shocked I lost my voice for a second." She bounced her index finger on the table in what seemed like a subconscious imitation of Detective Scott. "I didn't know how to respond, so I just stood up and said, 'I'm sorry. I can't.' Then I walked out of his office." She blinked back the tears in her eyes. "He can shut down the whole sheriff's office to me. Then where would I get my questions answered?"

I suspected that wasn't her real reason for being near tears. Detective Scott had always brought strong emotions out of her, I just didn't know why. "Did he say he wouldn't answer any more of your questions?"

"No," she said. "But I didn't give him a chance to say anything."

"I know he's persistent and obnoxiously pushy, but he doesn't strike me as vengeful." I reached across the table and patted her hand. "Why did you turn him down, anyway? You're both single."

She stared at me with her eyebrows raised. "You just said he's stubborn, pushy, and obnoxious. Why would I date him?"

"Because," I said.

"Because?"

"Well, why not?" I asked.

She gave me the smarty-pants smile that used to drive me nuts when we were in school. "Because. That's all I'm going to say."

Our server came and asked us if we were done. Abbie said yes. I said no. I wanted dessert. He took my order for biscochitos and carried our plates away.

"You're eating more than usual tonight," Abbie said.

"You can share the cookies with me."

"I hate them. Anise with cinnamon just doesn't do it for me."

I waved my hand in the air. "Don't try to change the subject. Why won't you go out with him? Do you dislike him that much?"

Her nostrils flared. "And you say *he's* pushy?" She took a deep breath. "Don't you remember why my ex-husband left me? He said I was too intense. Too absorbed in my work."

When she'd been married, Abbie worked as a journalist. Her husband was a cop. "You were both so young," I said. "You were both busy."

"I've only gotten more intense," she said, as though I hadn't spoken. "I don't want to . . ." She let her words fade as she picked up her napkin and shredded it into pieces.

I knew what she meant. Her husband had gotten sympathy from a couple of other women. She still blamed herself and was terribly afraid of another relationship.

"Abbie, you're older now. You really have changed."

The mustached server delivered my cookies and refilled my water and Abbie's tea.

"Yes. I'm worse." She shook her head. "I've been alone too long. I like my space and my apartment. I don't want to share. I don't have the time or nature to be a wife. And now his daughter is living with him? I could never be a stepmother."

"Well, I won't argue with you about that right now, even though I disagree, but for Pete's sake. Detective Scott just asked you out. He didn't ask you to marry him."

She had taken a big swallow of tea, started laughing, and gurgled instead. A few drops of liquid dripped down her chin. I picked up a napkin, reached across the table, and wiped her mouth. "That's better. You need to laugh." I paused. "So, are you going to go out with him?"

"No," she said. "No, I'm not. Can we drop it now?"

"There's more to this story, isn't there?"

"Trish . . ."

Her tight lips told me what I needed to know. She wasn't telling me everything, but I also recognized that she wasn't going to say another word tonight. That was fine. I'd find out one way or another.

Max wasn't home yet when Abbie dropped me at my house at eight. My mother delivered Charlie and Sammie at eight thirty. I felt out of sorts as I put the little kids to bed, wishing my husband were home.

"Granddad has a new calf," Charlie said

as I tucked him in.

"I love calves." I sat on the edge of his bed and wished I could run my fingers through his spiky red hair, but he wasn't keen about that kind of attention from me anymore. "They're so wobbly at first, then they start running around and jumping, acting like little kids on the playground."

Charlie rubbed his eyes. "I want cows when I grow up. I can work with Granddad. I'll be a farmer, too."

I smiled. "That would be great, honey." Even as I said the words, I thought about the hard life my father had lived. Only lately had he been able to relax because my mother was making good money at her doughnut shop. I also knew what Max's wealthy parents would think if any of their grandchildren went into farming. When I was dating Max, I overheard my mother-in-law say to him, "Farmers are fine, dear. We need them, but we don't need to date them." I was naive enough to think that as my relationship with Max grew, she would see that I made him happy and change her opinion. Boy, had I been naive.

But I never let her influence me, and I did my best to see that she didn't influence the children. As long as what they chose to do was honest and moral and made them happy, I would never dissuade them from their dreams, no matter what paths they chose.

A few minutes later, I finished praying with Sammie and was about to turn off her light and shut her door when she sat straight up in bed. Her blond hair fell over her face. "Mommy?"

"Yes?"

"Grandmom says she never sees you anymore."

There we have it. My mother's contribution to survival of the fittest. Evolution mother style. Traits handed from one generation to another. In this case, the fine art of manipulation.

"She says that all the time, sweetie. I'll call her tomorrow." I turned out the light.

"You prob'ly should." Sammie snuggled back under her covers. "She almost cried when she said it."

"Good night." I shut the door.

Back in the kitchen, I heard a car door slam, and a moment later, Karen, my stepdaughter, shot through the back door with her purse and a white bag in her hand.

She smiled at me and tossed the bag on the table. "Wow, Mom. I heard you and Tommy found Ms. Winters. You gonna solve the mystery?"

"I don't think your father would be thrilled about that." I already felt a little guilty about starting a clue notebook.

"You've gotta convince Dad to let you do it. You have to. At least we can trust you." Her expression turned grim.

"What do you mean by that?"

She put her purse on a chair and faced me. "Well, most of the kids don't think the cops are looking out for us. I mean, they searched Tommy's locker." She crossed her arms. "Oh please! Tommy?"

"The police aren't against you." I felt a bit hypocritical saying that given my own attitude toward a certain detective.

"They also suspect Mr. Slade. I mean, really. Mr. Slade? All you have to do is look at him to know he couldn't kill anybody. He's my favorite teacher."

While I was sympathetic because Marvin Slade had the kind of looks that made a woman want to take him home and feed him, I knew that had little to do with murderous intentions. "Some of the most innocent-looking people commit murder," I said.

"I know he didn't do it, but it looks bad for him."

"Why?"

"He and Ms. Winters haven't been getting

along." Karen stared at me. "Please, Mom."

"But that's good motivation for murder."

"Maybe, but I don't believe it," Karen said. "You have to do this."

Why did I feel this pressing need to investigate? Was it just Karen's request? Or was it because I had an insatiable curiosity and had been involved in a previous murder investigation? Or maybe I had some sort of crusader inside me that had to help the cops fight evil?

I sighed. I did have a sense of wanting to see justice done. That made my decision inevitable and meant that I was going to have to be honest with Max and tell him what I was going to do.

Karen could tell I was weakening. "I can let you know if I hear anything at school."

My stomach twisted. "No, Karen. Please. If this was murder, and it looks like it was, I don't want you involved."

She snorted. "The person who did it can't be anybody I know. Really." She caught my glance. "Oh, okay. As long as you promise to investigate."

"I promise, *if* Dad's okay with it," I said. "Now, how was work at the pretzel stand?"

"Cool. Brought you leftovers. I know how you like them." She pointed at the bag on the table.

"Thanks, honey."

"Well, I gotta finish my homework." She trotted from the room.

I slipped a cinnamon sugar pretzel from the bag, took a big bite, and chewed while I pondered Georgia's death from all angles. Then I caught myself reaching into the bag for a second pretzel and stopped. Overeating was developing into a bad habit. If I wasn't careful, I'd be the size of Texas by the time I had the baby. That wasn't normally a problem for me. When I wasn't pregnant, I had trouble remembering to eat. But when I was expecting, I could happily consume copious amounts of food all day. Eat and sleep. In fact, right now, the tiredness I'd fought all day was seeping into my bones, making me feel like jelly. I needed to get to bed even if Max wasn't home. And I'd take my Bible study with me. I'd get some work done before I fell asleep.

A while later, I woke to Max's beautiful face hovering over mine.

"Hi." He brushed the hair from my eyes and kissed me. Then he picked up my Bible and the study book from where they'd fallen on the bed beside me and placed them on the nightstand. "Guess you fell asleep doing this?"

"I fell asleep before I read the first word."

I tried to extricate my arms from the covers to pull him into a hug, but he stood up before I could.

"How are you?" he asked.

"Put out." My whine can rival Sammie's. "I had a special dinner planned for you tonight. I had steaks ready and arranged for the kids to be away."

He frowned and swiped his hand through his hair. "I'm sorry, but you should have told me earlier. I could have rearranged my meetings."

"I wanted to surprise you," I said.

He leaned over and kissed me again. For a minute, I thought he was going to be romantic, but he straightened and stepped back. "How are you feeling now? Are you okay about Georgia?"

"Abbie and I went out to dinner, so I talked with her about it. Right now I'm just achy and tired."

"Oh." He walked over to his dresser and pulled off his tie. "Well, I'm glad you're okay. I'm just sorry you had to be the one to find her."

"Well, it's not like it hasn't happened before."

"Don't remind me." He dropped the tie on the dresser.

I watched him with one eye because I was

having trouble keeping both open. "What's the big deal with all the meetings?"

He met my gaze briefly in the dresser mirror then turned and began to unbutton his shirt.

"Dad and I have several projects going on."

"More self-storage centers?"

"We're looking into that," he said.

Max and his father were building a self-storage empire that had started with our facility in Four Oaks.

"I'll be back in a minute," Max said. "Then we can finish talking."

Through almost closed eyelids, I watched him walk to the bathroom to take his shower. To say that Max is good-looking would be an understatement. Dark hair, green eyes, and chiseled cheeks and chin — he could be the cover model for a romance novel. And he looked good coming and going.

I heard the water in the shower start and decided I would try to resurrect my romantic evening. I wanted to cuddle with my husband. I settled back under the covers. My eyelids drifted shut. The next thing I felt was Max leaning over me to turn off the light. I tried to force my eyes open.

"Good night," he whispered and rolled

over with his back to me.

He obviously wasn't in the mood for cuddling, but I did need to tell him about my clue notebook. "Max?"

"Mmm?" He settled deeper under the blankets.

"You're not worried that I found Georgia Winters?"

He inhaled. I'd caught him off guard. He rolled over to face me. "Is there a reason I should be?"

"I'm collecting clues in a notebook." I held my breath.

He flopped onto his back. "I can't say I'm surprised."

"Detective Scott threatened me. He said he would tell you."

"If he thinks threats will work, he doesn't know you as well as I do." Max sounded resigned.

"Well, he was in a horrible mood. Did you know that he asked Abbie out?"

Max sighed. "What does him asking Abbie out have to do with you collecting clues?"

"Well, she turned him down."

"Okay . . . and?"

Max wasn't putting it all together. "Because of that, he was in a really bad mood."

Max grunted.

"And tonight Karen told me that Marvin

Slade is a suspect. She asked me to solve the mystery."

"The band teacher?"

"Yes, but how could he do it? As murderers go, he doesn't fit. He's just a skinny musician. Well, skinny or not, I guess he could have murdered someone, but if I had to pick someone right now, I'd be more inclined to think it was Carla. I'm sure she could take a grown man if she wanted to. Connie is more iffy, but a possibility." I paused and remembered something I'd need to add to my notebook. "You know what? Carla said that Connie and Georgia were fighting. And the football coach was around. He could have done it easily, but why would he kill her? Maybe he and Georgia were dating." I bit my lip and thought.

"There's a good chance it was a random crime, too," Max said. "Maybe drug related."

"Drugs?" The thought horrified me.

I heard the smile in his voice. "Honey, Four Oaks isn't Utopia. There's always a good possibility that someone was looking for something."

I chewed on the inside of my cheek. I wasn't having any trouble keeping my eyes open now. "My mother said it was a mob hit because a new housing development will eventually bring in gambling and all manner of crime. She actually used the word *avarice.*"

Max coughed then laughed. "Only your mother could come up with something like that."

"Yeah, I suppose."

We lay silently for a minute; then Max yawned and apologized. "Just promise me that you won't put yourself in danger. Last time was plenty for me."

"I never do that on purpose." I felt put out that he would think I was that stupid. "And I didn't find Georgia on purpose, either. I was just there for a play committee meeting. It's not like I go out looking for trouble."

He laughed. "You don't need to. It always finds you."

"Well, this time I don't think I have anything to worry about. I'm not a suspect. I hardly knew Georgia." I briefly thought about Tommy. "It's not like she was *my* teacher or anything."

"I'm not sure I like the idea of you collecting clues, but I'm not going to try to stop you. I don't think I could." He leaned over to kiss me again then rolled over on his side.

I was almost disappointed that he'd given in so quickly. I didn't want him to rampage like he had during the other murder investigation, but I wished he had tried a little harder to talk me out of it. I could have had fun with that. However, when he began snoring less than two minutes later, I realized he was exhausted.

So was I, but, perversely, now I was having trouble quieting my mind, which wandered from Georgia to Detective Scott and Abbie and finally to the housing development. My last thought was how so many times we think we know someone, or we understand a situation and have everything figured out, but we really don't. And that was exactly why it was going to be hard to figure out who murdered Georgia. No one is ever totally what he or she appears to be on the outside.

6

On Tuesday morning, Max got the little kids ready for school, and I fed them. While I ate breakfast, I pulled out my clue notebook and added, *Carla said Connie and Georgia were fighting. Were the coach and Georgia dating? Was it a random crime? Something to do with drugs?*

I half listened to the television, waiting for the local news, hoping to hear more about Georgia's death. A cheerful morning show host was running down national news, although what was considered important amazed me. She rambled on about the latest cell phone issues, including batteries that blow up. Then she mentioned the newest diet rage and a drug that helped erase bad memories and made coping with pressure easier, often used by musicians to enhance their concert performances.

"Now to the local news," she said. "The body of Four Oaks English teacher Georgia

Winters was discovered yesterday in the band room of Four Oaks High School. Local law enforcement will only say that the death is being treated as suspicious."

The picture on the screen cut to Carla in front of the school. She looked surprisingly good on television, but she said nothing I didn't already know, just that she and the authorities were doing everything in their power to keep the children safe.

I was relieved no one mentioned that I had found the body. I didn't want that kind of attention. If Carla's unwillingness to share had a positive side, it was that she wouldn't share the limelight with me.

I turned off the television. On Tuesday mornings, Max carpooled the little kids to school. I kissed everyone as he herded them out to his car. After they left, I went through five changes of clothes before I decided I didn't look good in anything. I gave up trying, yanked on a boring, tight pair of maternity jeans and an equally boring sweater, tucked my steno pad and some play advertising forms into my purse, and drove to Four Oaks Self-Storage. I was happy to run the accounting end of the business from my office at the Four Oaks facility, although I planned to take a leave of absence when I had the baby.

When I walked into the front office, Shirl, the office manager, was talking on the phone. She waved at me to wait until she was done. I plunked my purse on the counter.

After she'd slapped the receiver down, she turned to face me. "I heard about that Winters woman."

I was sure everyone within a hundred-mile radius had heard about the Winters woman.

"So, are you going to solve this mystery?" Shirl asked.

"I'm not sure," I said, even as I removed the notebook from my bag.

She opened a drawer in her desk, pulled out a tube of Avon extra-moisturizing hand lotion, and squirted some into her palm.

"Do you know anything?" I lifted a pen from the desktop and held it poised over the pad.

She shrugged, rubbing her hands together. "Well, Sue, my neighbor's daughter's sister-in-law, works at the school." Shirl's eyes glittered, and I could tell she was just winding up.

"Well, I'll tell you what." Shirl put the lotion away, pulled an emery board from the pencil holder, and began sawing at her nails. "No one is surprised someone bopped that woman. She's got mean as a snake lately. I figure it's probably early menopause. She should have gotten some help. Got some herbs. You know, like black cobash?"

"I think that's black cohash."

Shirl waved a dismissive hand. "Whatever. You do realize that if more people used herbs, the drug companies would have to start charging less for their pills."

"Uh-huh." I wondered what she'd been reading.

"It's true," Shirl said. "That new pharmacist in town sells all sorts of natural stuff. You'd think he'd be afraid of losing money, but he's always giving out advice. And that Georgia needed some kind of help. You do know she threatened to fail Jason."

I shook my head. "I didn't —"

"Jason is the star quarterback on the Four Oaks High School football team. He fails? He's off the team. He goes? The season goes. That happens? Coach Smith probably loses his position."

I snorted. "Well, how stupid is that? Firing a coach because a kid fails. After all, it's just a game —"

Oops. Shirl tapped the nail file against her palm and stared at me as if I'd just uttered blasphemy. "Our team hasn't had a losing season in five years," she said icily.

Our team. Like high school football was

the be-all and end-all of life. I hadn't understood that level of enthusiasm when I was in high school. Now that I'm an adult, I understand it even less. But this did give the coach a good reason to be a suspect.

A car pulled up in the parking lot. Shirl stared over the counter and through the window. My gaze followed hers.

"That's Connie, the costume lady," Shirl told me.

I didn't bother to remind her that I knew Connie, too, and could easily recognize her from fifteen feet away.

Shirl plunked the nail file back into the pencil holder and thumbed through some paperwork on her desk. "She called me yesterday and said you said I should hold a unit for her. She just bought a whole slew of new costumes." Shirl picked up the lease she'd already printed out and put it and a pen on the counter. "You know she's related to Georgia, don't you? Cousin. She left town right after high school. I don't know what happened, but she moved back here not so long ago."

Somewhere in the recesses of my memory, I realized I did know that. That made me even more curious to know why she and Georgia had been fighting.

The bell over the door rang when Connie

walked in. Her eyes were red-rimmed.

"I was surprised you came out today," Shirl said. "I wouldn't be able to function if one of my relatives was murdered."

Connie's face blanched.

"I'm so sorry," I said with double meaning. Even though Connie's name was on my suspect list, I was sorry for her loss. And for Shirl's lack of tact.

"Thank you." Connie sniffled. "I'm sure it was difficult for you . . . finding her."

"Yes, very." I drew in a breath, trying not to remember Georgia on the floor. "Were you at the school when the police arrived?"

"No." Her eyes filled with tears. "I left right after I talked with you."

"Well, it's a good thing you didn't walk down to the band room with Trish," Shirl said. "I can't imagine how horrible it would be to find a relative bludgeoned to death."

If it were possible, Connie's face became whiter.

"Did the police bang on your door and tell you she died?" As usual, Shirl was a bull in a china shop.

Connie sniffled again. "Yes. They went out to the farm. It was horrible. Granny Nettie was there. It was the worst way she could have heard about it, although I'm not sure how much she really understood."

"I'm sorry," I said again.

"Thank you." She pulled her checkbook from her purse. "Well, work helps me cope. Besides, I have to get all this stuff into storage. I'm going to be really busy now."

"Oh?" Shirl shoved the lease toward Connie.

"Someone has to care for Granny Nettie." She swiped a tear from her cheek with the back of her hand. "You know she hasn't been doing so well in the last year. Georgia was caring for her. I helped during the day while Georgia was at work."

"I heard Nettie wasn't well," Shirl said. "What's wrong with her?"

"Mostly old age." Connie signed the lease, wrote a check, and handed both to Shirl. "Georgia was cracking under the pressure, but now she . . ." More tears. "She was having a rough time of it all."

"I can understand," I said.

"That's probably why she was acting the way she was," Shirl said. "A shrew."

"Shirl!" Sometimes I wanted to stuff a sock in her mouth.

She waved a pen in the air. "Well, people talk." She looked at Connie. "I know you heard what they were saying."

She nodded. "Yes. Georgia was ornery lately. It was because of all the pressure."

97

She stopped suddenly and took a deep breath. "I haven't been feeling that well. My heart keeps pounding. I think it's stress."

I felt guilty for having Connie on my list of suspects. She was obviously miserable. Still, that meant nothing. I was pretty sure that some murderers felt remorse.

"You know, there's things to help that," Shirl said authoritatively. "Herbal remedies. I can get you some." She eyed Connie. "But Nettie used to make all that sort of stuff. She'd know what to do. She used to grow her own herbs."

Connie picked up her purse. "We all drink her herbal tea. It's got ginseng in it."

"Gotta be careful with herbs, though," Shirl said. "Pick the wrong ones and . . ." She ran her finger across her neck.

Once again, I wondered what Shirl had been reading — or drinking. This herbal thing was a brand-new topic for her, and I had a feeling I'd be hearing more about it before she got it out of her system.

Connie backed toward the door. "Well, I should get this stuff unloaded. I've got so much to do."

Shirl clucked sympathetically as Connie left the office. We watched her car drive up the parking lot to her new unit.

"Lover's quarrel," Shirl said.

"What?" Sometimes talking to Shirl made my brain felt like it was in a wringer washer.

"A crime of passion. Maybe Marvin or Coach Smith was dating Georgia. And then she broke up with him."

"Seems sort of obvious," I said.

"Isn't it always when it involves love gone bad? People just lose control. Then they murder in cold blood."

I shrugged. "Maybe." Another customer came in, so I went to my office. There, I pulled out my steno pad to make notes.

Were Georgia and the coach dating? Did he clobber her?

I chewed my pen. Another important part of solving a crime is looking into the victim's past. Connie had said some interesting things about Georgia.

Georgia lived with Nettie. Was she overwhelmed taking care of her?

At the familiar sound of a purring engine, I looked out the window. Max pulled into the parking lot. I was surprised to see him. He hadn't said anything about coming into the office today. The bell over the door rang as he came inside.

"Hi, Mr. C.," Shirl said. "I didn't expect you today."

"Good morning. Just need to pick up something I forgot. Any messages?"

99

"Yes. Your *mother* called. Then your father called. Then your *mother* called again." Shirl felt the same as I did about Max's mother, and that was obvious by her slightly sarcastic emphasis on *mother.*

"Okay. I'll call her in a minute."

He entered my office smiling and kissed me. "You okay?"

"Yeah, especially now," I said. "This is a nice surprise."

He grinned, but it faded when he noticed my notebook. "Clues?"

"Mmm-hmm."

"You're incorrigible."

"Probably."

"That's why I love you, though." His grin returned.

"Because I'm incorrigible?"

"Because being married to you keeps life from becoming boring." He kissed me again, this time longer, and I felt it all the way to my toes.

When he was done, I couldn't speak.

He stepped back and winked at me. He knows exactly how he affects me. "Anyway, I have a couple of things to do. Is that Connie Gilbert I see unloading things?"

I nodded. "Did you know she's related to Georgia?"

Max nodded. I shouldn't have been surprised. He seems to know everybody and everything.

"I was a little shocked that she was out so soon after Georgia's death," I said, "but she's got a bunch of costumes to store. She says she has to take care of Nettie now. Connie doesn't seem to be doing very well."

"I can understand," he said. "Does she have help unloading?"

"Not right now."

"*Hmm.* It looked like she has some heavier boxes. I'll go give her a hand for a couple of minutes."

"That's sweet of you. You want me to come?"

He shook his head. "I don't want you lifting anything."

I settled down to work. Max returned twenty minutes later and disappeared into his office. I needed to get busy getting advertising commitments for the play program. I'd have Max fill out a form for Cunningham & Son. I'd fill out one for Four Oaks Self-Storage.

I took one of the forms and went to Max's office. His door was open a crack, so I pushed it and walked in. He was on the phone and looked up with a frown, holding up a finger to tell me to wait.

He shoved some papers around on his

desk. I narrowed my eyes in suspicion. Because of who I am, how I am, and how I've always been, I recognize a cover-up when I see it. That's because I have the regrettable ability to cover up with the best of them. Something I'm working hard to change.

He mumbled a few uh-huhs then said good-bye and hung up. "I'm sorry, baby. I'm in a hurry to finish something here." As he spoke, he placed a leather portfolio on the desk in front of him over the papers. "I've got a lot to do, and I hadn't planned to come to the office today. I have one more phone call to make. Can you give me just a couple minutes?"

That meant he wanted me to leave. I sighed my objection, but he ignored it and just stared at me.

"Okay. Well, I'll be in my office." I didn't move.

"Great. I'll be there in a minute. And would you please shut the door on your way out?" He picked up the phone again.

I knew when I was defeated. I turned and shut his office door. What was he hiding from me?

At my desk, I watched the lights on the phones. Not too long after Max's turned dark, I heard him leave his office and shut the door.

He appeared in my office. "I have to get going."

"I need you to fill out this form for advertising for Cunningham & Son." I held it out to him.

He put down his briefcase, crossed the room, and took the form and flipped through the pages. "All this for advertising in a school play program?"

"Yep," I said. "That's Carla. Obsessive."

"I'll say." He stuck the form in his briefcase.

"Max, is everything okay?"

He pecked me on the cheek. So different from the passionate kiss of a few minutes before.

"Yes. I'll be home tonight, hopefully at the normal time. I told Tommy that Sherry could come over to dinner tonight. They want to practice for the play."

I wanted to say, "Thanks for asking me first," but I didn't. I just nodded. He turned and left. I didn't understand. One minute he was kissing me with feeling; the next he was like a cold fish. What was going on? I buried my nose in work, trying to ignore my swirling thoughts. Then Shirl hollered from the outer office that she was going out to lunch, emphasizing she had an important appointment.

Normally I would have been curious, because Shirl never goes out to lunch. Instead, she frugally packs a sandwich, which she eats in the conference room in front of a tiny television we had installed for her. There she reads a romance book while she watches her favorite soap opera.

Today, however, I was too busy wondering what Max was hiding to think about Shirl. When her car pulled from the lot, the war began. Bad Trish began to argue with Good Trish.

I wanted to search Max's desk to see if he had left anything behind that would give me a hint about what he was hiding. I could temporarily turn off the security cameras and lock the front door so I wouldn't be caught.

I took a step toward the front door then stopped.

My mother raised me on clichés. They still live in my brain and come back to me in her voice at the appropriate moments. Like when you hear an annoying song on the radio, and the dumbest line in the whole thing repeats itself over and over again in your mind until you think you'll go crazy.

I could hear my mother speaking right now. *"Trish, one day your curiosity is going to get the best of you. You know what they say, don't you? Curiosity killed the cat."* When she told me things like that, she added object lessons when she could, like smashed cats in the road. *"See?"* She'd point with great enthusiasm. *"That cat just* had *to cross the road. Too busy being curious to watch for cars."*

Yes, but this is my husband. I argued pointlessly with her in my head. *He shouldn't keep secrets from me. I'm not a cat, and I'm not crossing the road.*

I looked around the empty office. I didn't have to worry about being smashed by a car unless someone accidentally came barreling through the front window.

No one would ever know. Except me and God.

7

Good Trish triumphed over Bad Trish. I didn't search Max's office. To reward myself, I got three different flavors of ice cream when I stopped by the Shopper's Super Saver after work to pick up things for dinner.

At the checkout, a young man with more piercings and tattoos than I cared to look at was shoving my purchases into plastic bags with abandon.

"Um, those are eggs there," I said.

"Sure are." He crammed more items into the bag.

I was too tired to argue. Besides, trying to write my check and simultaneously recall whether I had hot fudge at home for the ice cream was daunting enough. That's when I heard Georgia's murder being discussed with great relish at the checkout behind me.

". . . We've never had a tragedy like this at my school before, and I don't intend for it to ever happen again."

I recognized Carla Bickford's voice and turned around to look at her. She was holding court two checkouts down from me like the queen of England, with a sensible purse that coordinated with her proper suit. The whole outfit was an echo of what she'd been wearing the day before.

She met my gaze, and her eyes widened. "Why, Trish. I didn't recognize you from behind."

What did that mean? Was my behind different than it used to be? Had I gained so much pregnancy weight that I'd become unrecognizable? Or did it mean she just never really saw me from this angle before?

With a small wave of her hand, Carla motioned toward me then gazed slowly from person to person, acknowledging her subjects. "Trish is the one who found Georgia."

Everyone's eyes fell on me. The low, confiding pitch of Carla's voice had given her words just enough drama that I wouldn't have been surprised to hear everyone ooh and aah.

I recognized one of my mother's friends in line, and she nodded and smiled at me, as though I had done something terribly special by finding a dead woman.

"Oh wow," my cashier said.

"Dude," the bagger said, looking at me with a sudden new respect in his eyes.

I felt like saying, "Aw, shucks, 'tweren't nothin'."

"Did you throw up?" my cashier asked me breathlessly.

"No." I hated this kind of attention, particularly since it was at Georgia's expense.

My mother's friend had to add her two cents. "Well, everyone should remember that Trish is the one who found Jim Bob in the milk case last spring. She's used to this by now."

"Dude!" the bagger eyed me with awe and carefully bagged the rest of my groceries.

What a thing to be known for. Finding dead people.

My mother's friend wasn't done. "Not only that, but she solves crimes."

"Well, not exactly," I said.

"That's not what your mother says."

The air stilled, as if all the people around me were holding their breath. All eyes were on me. I wanted to disappear. Solving crimes was one thing, but to have the fact advertised all over the county could be dangerous.

"So will you cancel the play?" a woman in

line behind Carla asked her.

That got everyone's focus off of me.

"Absolutely not," Carla said. "The show must go on. We can't let anything take us from our duties."

I waited for applause, but it wasn't forthcoming.

Carla sniffed, put her purse strap over her shoulder, and picked up her grocery bag. "We need to get to the bottom of this crime. I'm upping the security in the school. I told the school board at the beginning of the year that we were at risk and needed a school resource officer. We also need cameras in the halls. You never know when a crazy person is going to break in and hold the children hostage. Now I have proof that we are susceptible to attack from the outside."

That was the third time I'd heard someone say a stranger had broken into the school. Was I the only one who didn't believe that?

The bagger dude offered to push my groceries outside to my car. I agreed and ended up walking next to Carla. "So you think a stranger broke into the school?"

"Certainly. You don't think anybody we know could be guilty of this, do you?" Her gaze was challenging.

I shrugged and decided not to give her

my opinion at the moment. "Did you know Georgia well? I didn't, although she did grow up around here."

"Well, I knew her better than the other teachers on staff. We ate dinner together on occasion. She was dedicated. Determined that the children should be well educated." Carla's purse slipped off her shoulder, and she shoved it back. "She was under a great deal of pressure to take care of her grandmother, though. I wondered if she should take a leave of absence."

"Did you know that she and Connie were cousins?" I asked.

Carla blinked. "Well, of course I knew that." She stopped in front of a gray Volvo and opened the front door, leaning over and placing her bag on the passenger seat.

Bagger Dude hovered behind me, listening.

"Aren't you worried about the football team?" I asked.

"The football team?" Carla stood up, gripping her purse with both hands, and stared down at me. "Why? Just like our band, our football team is one of the best in the tri-county area. As a result, we get attention from some of the best colleges in the area."

Rah, rah, rah. Sis boom bah. I was getting the party line and decided to grab the bull by the horns, to quote another one of my mother's oft-used clichés. "Well, I heard that Georgia was threatening to fail Jason, who is the star quarterback. Wouldn't it be possible that he or Coach Smith had something to do with the attack on Georgia?"

"What?" Carla blinked like a toad in a hailstorm.

I'd plainly caught her off guard, so I pressed my advantage. "I heard that Jason was going to be removed from the team."

She took two steps backward. "It's absolutely ridiculous to think our football team is good only because of one player. Besides, if Jason could be guilty, then any number of our other young people could be guilty." She took several deep breaths. "That would mean her death was some kind of personal vendetta. . . . No, I'm sure this was a stranger."

I thought she was protesting too much. "Well, you never really know what people are going to do. There are rumors —"

"Hearsay," Carla snapped. "You shouldn't be listening to it." A red flush worked up her cheeks. "I don't care if you *do* solve mysteries."

Her hostility seemed a bit over the top to me. Still, I didn't want to stress her out any more than I already had. I forced myself to laugh. "Yep, gossip can be a killer, all right. Especially in a small town."

She visibly relaxed. "Remember our re-scheduled meeting tomorrow afternoon. I don't want anything to distract us from our goals. I want to discuss the advertising for the school play. I'd like to see the paid ads throughout the program. And I want the whole thing professionally printed on heavy, good quality paper."

I nodded even though I thought the idea was ridiculous. This was a school play in a public school, for Pete's sake. But what did I know?

"This will raise money for the drama club as well as present our high school in a good light." Carla slipped into the driver's seat. "I'll see you tomorrow afternoon at the meeting."

I turned away and wondered what was wrong with our high school that it had to be presented in such a good light. Well, other than the fact that it had been the scene of a murder.

My spiky-haired bagger followed me to my car with my basket. "Dude, that woman is a freak."

"What?"

He motioned with his head at the back end of Carla's car as she pulled out of the parking lot. "Her. She's a freak."

"How come?" We halted at the back of my SUV, and I popped the back door open.

"Too good for everyone. You know? Like those old bags on the BBC." He started loading my groceries. "She acts like she's on drugs, man."

I had a feeling he would know.

"You know what they say about the coach, don't you?" He turned to stare at me.

"No."

"Steroids."

I stared at him in disbelief. "Steroids? You can't be serious."

"Serious as a heart attack." He shrugged. "Took 'em a long time. Affected his head." He tapped his temple then slammed the car door shut. "Now he makes sure his players do well on tests, if you get my drift."

"Steroids?" I asked. "Do they help on tests?"

He laughed and stared at me. I felt uncomfortable under his scrutiny. "He has other ways."

"How do you know this?" I asked.

His eyes narrowed. "I hear things. Listen, I gotta get back to work."

"Okay." I turned to my SUV and used the remote to open the locks.

"Hey, lady."

I turned.

Bagger Dude scratched his arm. "Be careful about askin' questions." He swiveled on his sneakered foot and headed back to the store.

That sounded like a threat. I shivered, got into the car, and locked my doors. I needed to write down what I'd just heard. I pulled a pen and my steno pad from my purse.

Bagger Dude says Coach used steroids and they messed up his head. He arranges for players to pass tests in order to stay on the team. How?

Carla is defensive. Team isn't dependent on just one player. I stopped and thought carefully about her words. *Carla never denied that Jason or the coach had done anything wrong. But she insists that it was a stranger who killed Georgia.*

After staring at the words, I shut the steno pad and tucked it in my purse, along with the pen. As I started my SUV, I noticed my wedding rings needed to be cleaned. That's when it dawned on me that Carla hadn't been wearing any rings. Not even an engagement ring. Strange. I thought she had a fiancé.

I drove home, mentally reviewing all of my clues. Murder investigations have a way of peeling away people's veneer of civility.

Before I was done, I was going to know some people in my town a lot better than they wanted to be known.

Water flew from my salad spinner as I twirled it in the kitchen sink. I had my Bible study open on the counter, trying to meditate on the Scripture. *Be on your guard; stand firm in the faith; be men of courage, be strong. Do everything in love.* As I thought about that, the back door opened. I turned. Tommy and Sherry walked into the room frowning, bringing with them a dark atmosphere of despair.

Sherry met my eyes. "Hello, Mrs. Cunningham."

"Hey, Mom," Tommy said.

Neither smiled.

"I hope you like steak, Sherry." I needed to use the steaks I'd thawed the night before, so I had bought a couple more for dinner tonight. They were cooking on the gas grill out on the patio, manned by Max, who was in slightly better spirits. At least he'd seemed that way when he pulled me into an enthusiastic kiss a few minutes ago that ended only when Sammie interrupted us.

Sherry offered to help me, and Tommy left to take his books to his room. Karen came traipsing in and gave Sherry and me a hand carrying things to the table.

In a couple of minutes, we were all seated at the dining room table except Charlie. He came straggling in, a sour expression on his face.

"You okay?" I asked as he sat down.

"Yeah," he mumbled.

Max asked the blessing. For a few minutes, no one said a word. Tommy and Sherry kept exchanging glances; then Sherry dropped her fork on her plate with a clatter.

"I'm going to ask her, Tommy."

His knuckles turned white on his water glass. "Sherry, remember?"

"I know I promised, but she can help us. You're the one who told me she's great at solving mysteries."

Max stopped chewing.

"I already asked her to do it last night," Karen said.

Charlie looked up, and for the first time since he entered the room, his eyes lit up. "You gonna ask Mom to help you solve a mystery? She can do it, you know, no matter what anybody says."

Sammie grinned. "Yeah, Mommy can help."

I couldn't resist. "What do you guys need help with?"

Tommy was frowning at Sherry in exactly the same way Max was at me, glittery green eyes with creases between the brows.

"I've got to do it. I'm sorry." Sherry turned teary eyes to me. "Tommy is a suspect in the attack on Ms. Winters."

"What?" Max's gaze fell on me and then slid to his eldest son. "Tommy?"

Tommy glared at Sherry. "I told you to wait until I talked to Dad."

She waved a hand in the air. "I overheard Corporal Fletcher. And my dad is coming to get me after dinner because my car's in the shop. He doesn't . . . want Tommy to drive me home. I think it's because he wonders if Tommy did it."

"Is this true?" Max asked softly, glancing at me. I knew what he was thinking. He wondered if I knew and hadn't told him. I wasn't fooled by the tone of his voice. He speaks very softly when he's really upset.

"You can't really be a suspect. You just happened to be there, right?" I looked at our eldest. He wouldn't meet my gaze.

Charlie bounced in his chair. "Well, Deep Freeze Winters didn't like you much, did she?"

I turned to him. "You called her Deep Freeze?"

"That's what Tommy and everyone called

her. Because of her last name. Winters."
Charlie sounded as though that was the
coolest thing in the world, no pun intended.

I didn't have time to consider that, because Sherry was very near hyperventilation
as she reached across the table to grab at
my hand. "Please, Mrs. Cunningham."

I squeezed her hand while I tried to
untangle my thoughts. *Tommy had absolutely
no motivation in the world to kill Georgia . . .
right?*

Max cleared his throat. "Why would Eric,
uh, Detective Scott, be looking at Tommy
as a suspect? Why didn't someone tell me
about this?" He favored me with a quick,
narrow-eyed stare that made me feel defensive.

"Last night on the phone, I told you they
had interviewed Tommy. You said it didn't
matter. They were doing that to everyone. I
mean, how could Tommy be a real suspect?"
My voice got louder. "If I haven't learned
anything else, I've learned that a good
suspect has to have a good motive. That's
the key factor in solving crimes, you know.
Motivation. Well, motivation and . . . acces-
sibility."

Tommy, Sherry, and Karen stared at me. I
could have sworn they weren't breathing.
Then a chill made the hair on my arms

stand up, because I realized they knew something I didn't.

Max leaned forward. "Son?"

Sherry and Tommy exchanged glances. "Tell them, Tommy. If you don't, I will."

Tommy's shoulders sagged. "Well, Ms. Winters said I helped Jason cheat on an English exam. That's why I was looking for her the day she was killed. I wanted to tell her I didn't do it."

"What?" Max and I both said.

Sherry slapped her hand on the table. "He didn't cheat. Neither did Jason. The problem was we studied together, so our answers were similar. She said she wasn't going to let Tommy be in the play. Maybe get him expelled. And she was going to get Jason kicked off the football team."

Max was breathing harder across the table.

"What's 'expelled,' Mommy?" Sammie asked.

"Kicked out of school," I said absentmindedly. Even though I was on the verge of panic, the accusation made no sense to me. Why would Georgia think Tommy was guilty and not Sherry — not that I wanted Sherry expelled either, for several reasons. One, I liked her. Two, she wasn't guilty. Three, her father would blame Tommy, and vicariously, I would be to blame, too.

I turned to the teenagers. "Is this because of Coach Smith?"

The teenagers looked at each other.

"What are you talking about?" Max asked me.

"I heard he arranges for his players to get good grades." All three teenagers were staring at the table. I wanted to say something about the drugs, but I'd wait until I talked to Max. "Why was Georgia Winters fixated on Tommy?"

Max glanced at me then turned back to the kids.

Tommy finally looked up. "I don't know. She used to like me."

Sherry met my gaze, and I read a silent plea.

"This could really mess up my college plans," Tommy said.

I felt as close to hyperventilation as Sherry was acting. Yes, cheating would certainly mess up Tommy's college plans. So would being accused of Georgia's murder.

Max stood and told Tommy to meet him in his office. Charlie scampered upstairs to his room. Sammie followed him with a purposeful look on her face. I had a feeling she wanted him to explain to her more about what was going on. She figured Charlie would know because he loved crime and detective shows. Karen and Sherry carried leftovers into the kitchen.

I stacked dirty dinner plates at the dining room table, ignoring my husband, who was standing next to his chair. I didn't like his body language, which was all stiff like a mad dog. "Trish —"

"Max, don't say a word. I'm just keeping clues in a notebook." I began to gather up silverware. "I didn't know any of this. But I heard something today about drug use, too. That Coach Smith used drugs to help his players."

Max was breathing hard again. "Was that from a reliable source?"

I thought about Bagger Dude. "No, probably not."

"Sherry shouldn't have asked you to investigate. Her father is the detective." Max shook his head. "I thought Tommy was with you when you discovered Georgia."

I looked up at him. "Well, he was. Sort of. I mean, he got there after I got there. I don't know where he'd been. I really didn't think it was that big a deal." I gulped. "This looks bad, Max. I can't honestly say that Tommy didn't do it, although I *know* he didn't."

Max had a hard, cold look in his eyes that I rarely saw. "I need to go talk to Tommy. We'll be in my office." He whirled on his heel and strode down the hall.

The older girls helped me clean the kitchen. None of us spoke. I was surprised that Sherry stayed, since it appeared Tommy would be busy the rest of the evening, but she lingered even after the dishes were done and Karen had left the room.

"I thought your dad was coming to get you," I said.

"He is, shortly." She crossed her arms. "I wanted to talk to you alone, though."

"Okay." I motioned to the kitchen table. I hoped this wasn't going to be something like a confession of true love for my son. I wasn't ready for anything like that. But my worry was squelched when I saw a steely flash in her eyes. The look wasn't that of a young lady about to announce her true love.

As we sat down, I studied her face. She had the angular look of Detective Scott, but her bones were finer. She still hadn't grown into her features, and she would never be a classic beauty, but I could tell that when she hit her midtwenties, men would be falling all over her.

She placed her elbows on the table and clasped her hands together as if in supplication. "Mrs. Cunningham, please solve this mystery."

"Call me Mrs. C.," I said to distract her,

because I didn't know how to reply.

She nodded. "Okay, but please? Solve the mystery."

"Sherry, you know your dad doesn't want me involved." I wasn't about to tell her I was already keeping notes. Her intense gaze made me uneasy. My fingers danced a rhythm on the table while I tried to figure a way out of this conversation.

"My dad can be pretty pushy," she admitted.

"That's putting it mildly," I murmured, hoping I would never again have another interview session with him.

"Yeah, and he really likes to get confessions out of people. He took classes to learn how to do that." She sighed. "I've never been able to keep the truth from him — at least in the long run. Sometimes being a cop's kid is really, really hard. I mean, I have to live up to all these *standards*. Even when I wasn't living with him. Now it's worse."

I could only imagine. And to make things harder, her mom wasn't around to balance things out. "I understand he's tough. We've had, uh, discussions in the past."

She returned my smile. "Well, he has made a couple comments about the Cunningham stubbornness."

I felt a brief sense of accomplishment that

the bullheaded detective thought I was worthy of comment.

"My dad is a really good cop," she said. "I can admit that, even if I don't want to live with him. But see, he can't find out things like you can. People treat cops differently than they would regular folks. Honestly, cops act different, too." She paused and eyed me. "And I'm in an even better place to find out things. We could work together. You and me."

I stared at her in disbelief. "No way. Not only is that unsafe, but your father would find a reason to lock me up and throw away the key." I stood, placed my hands flat on the table, and stared down at her. "At the very least, he'd accuse me of contributing to your delinquency."

"Well, then, let's hope he doesn't find out." She stood, too, and faced me across the table. "I've thought a lot about this. My aunt is at our house, and that's distracting my dad. She could be a problem, but I can work around her. I have to go to school anyway. That's where I'm going to look for things."

"I don't —"

"How can it be dangerous?" she continued. "I'll just be listening. Most adults don't pay attention to kids, and they say a lot of things when they think we're not listening. I could start writing things down like Tommy says you do, and we could compare notes."

So much for not telling her about my notebook. I wanted to shake her. Was this how frustrated Max felt with me sometimes? Tiredness hit me. I needed to sleep. I'd be able to think better tomorrow morning.

I met her gaze. "No, I can't let you do it. It's bad enough for adults."

Sherry lifted her chin. "Actually, I'm eighteen. I *am* an adult."

At my frown, she nodded. "It's true. Because of the divorce and all, I repeated first grade."

"That doesn't mean your father won't be mad when he finds out. And, believe me, somehow he'll find out. It also doesn't mean that you'll be safe. I'll feel responsible."

She leaned across the table, facing me nose to nose. "Mrs. C., if you won't let me help you, I'm doing it myself. No one is going to stop me."

In the end, what could I say?

8

"So Cunningham & Son will buy an ad for the program, right?" I asked Max as he passed through the kitchen behind me.

He grunted in the affirmative.

"Are you still mad at me?" I shoved the last of the dirty cereal bowls into the dishwasher.

"I was never mad at you."

"Well, irritated, then?" I turned to face him.

He was standing by the door to the garage dressed in his usual Wednesday navy pinstripe power suit. Normally it made me want to loosen his red tie and smother him with kisses, but today he looked icy and formidable. "I just wish someone had told me that the police suspected Tommy."

I opened my mouth to protest, and he raised his hands in a gesture of surrender.

"I understand what you said. I guess there's no way you could have known that

Tommy was a serious suspect. I'm not blaming you."

"But you're irritated with me."

He frowned. "Why would you say that?"

I crossed my arms. "You hardly talked to me last night. You didn't even kiss me good night."

That's when he finally smiled. "Honey, you went to bed early while I was still talking to Tommy. You were sound asleep when I came upstairs. I did kiss you; you just didn't wake up."

That was no excuse, as far as I was concerned. "So you're going to talk to Carla today about Tommy cheating?" I turned and shut the dishwasher door harder than I intended. "I can do it, you know. Besides, I'm mad at her because she didn't say anything to me about all this yesterday at the store."

"I'm sure you could talk to her just fine, but I'll take care of it." I glanced at him over my shoulder, and he raised an eyebrow. I knew he was thinking he didn't want to set me loose on Carla. That was wise. "I don't need any help, okay? And I don't think you should be involved anymore. Knowing that Eric is seriously looking at Tommy and some of the other people at the school as suspects scares me. It's probable the murderer isn't just some stranger who happened to be passing by."

At last. Someone saw the crime the way I did. I pulled the kids' lunches from the refrigerator. "Do you remember when I was investigating Jim Bob's murder?"

"That would be hard to forget," he murmured in a facetious tone I couldn't miss.

I ignored that and pressed my point while I slipped cookies into each lunch container. "Well, after you got all obsessive about me doing that, and we had a huge fight, you said you were going to stop being so bossy and overbearing."

"Yes, I know, but that was before . . ." His voice drifted off.

I dropped the last package of cookies into the lunches and turned to face him. "Before what?"

He inhaled and averted his gaze. "Before Tommy was involved."

"And you don't think that's a good reason for me to help?" I planted my hands on my hips. "Lots of people think I have a talent for being a sleuth. My mother, for one."

Max closed his eyes for a moment and took a deep breath. He opened them again. "Trish, I'm positive that you're a good sleuth. You have that sort of mind. But right now, you're pregnant."

"Max, we agreed the night before last. I've already started my clue notebook. I can sleuth and not be in danger."

A grim smile flashed across his lips. "And pigs fly."

Hearing a cliché of my mother's coming from the mouth of my sophisticated husband made me laugh. "You don't need to worry. I have plans."

His nostrils flared. "Plans? Like what kind of plans?"

"I'm getting off work early today for a play committee meeting. But before I go to the school, I'm going to Ma's shop to ask her to buy a full-page ad in the school play program. I also want to see if she's heard anything that would be useful. Then I'm going to buy doughnuts to take to the meeting. You know the effect my mother's doughnuts have on people. Makes them giddy. Maybe someone will talk." I met his gaze. "That should be harmless enough."

"Right." He eyed me. "Will all the main suspects be there?"

"Well, the football team and the football coach won't be there." I stared at him. "But lots of other people will be there."

"You mean lots of other *suspects* will be there." He sighed. "Oh, all right. I'm not going to be able to stop you, anyway." The wrinkles on his forehead deepened.

"Is anything else wrong?" I asked.

He picked up his briefcase. "Isn't the problem with Tommy enough?"

I relented, walked over, and kissed him. "Don't worry, Max. Everything will be fine."

"I wish I could believe that," he said.

Doris's Doughnuts are a favorite with everyone, from construction workers to cops. My mother started the business years ago in a little strip mall, selling coffee and doughnuts made from recipes perfected when I was just a tot. Now she has added other pastries, along with breakfast and lunch sandwiches.

When I pulled up, I could see that she had plenty of customers, even though it was after lunch. I grabbed my purse, crawled from my SUV, and took a deep breath to prepare myself to enter the fray.

Over half the tables in the dining area were filled, and heads turned when I walked through the door. A few people waved. Gail, my mother's best friend and right-hand gal, was stacking blue coffee mugs behind the counter.

She looked up and stared at me. "Doris," she yelled. "You'd never believe who just walked in." Her voice was loud enough for people out in the parking lot to hear her.

"Who?" My mother's equally loud voice roared from the back room.

I braced myself for what was coming.

Gail cocked an ample hip against the counter. "I'm not sure I remember her name. It's been so long."

"Oh, come on." April May Winters, my mother's left-hand gal, paused in the midst of making an espresso. "Don't give her a hard time." She smiled at me, her bright hazel eyes sparkling.

Something niggled at my brain about April — something my mother had said — but I didn't have a chance to explore my thoughts, because my mother walked out of the back room, mouth first, wiping her hands on a towel.

". . . must mean my daughter. Although I don't know if I would even recognize her. I haven't seen her in so long. I talk to her friend Abbie more than I talk to her. *She's* coming to dinner on Friday."

I took a deep breath. "Hi, Ma. You know we'll be at your house on Friday, too."

She slapped the towel down on the counter, crossed her arms, and glared at me. I'd seen her just the previous weekend, but she conveniently didn't mention that. For a short time after Jim Bob's murder was solved, I'd been in her good graces. She was proud that I had, as she put it, single-handedly solved the murder for the police. I hadn't, of course, but no one can convince my mother of anything she doesn't want to believe. My notoriety wore off after a couple of weeks, and things returned to normal, which meant she was back to manipulation and minor insults. But her present glare was not normal.

I leaned my elbows on the counter and stared down through the glass at the fatty circles. "I need two dozen doughnuts. Your choice." I eyed my mother and lowered my voice. "What's wrong, Ma?"

Gail harrumphed, grabbed a box, and snatched up doughnuts like she was picking Japanese beetles from a prize rosebush.

"I heard Tommy is a suspect in the attack on Georgia Winters," Ma said in a loud voice. "The police questioned him. And you didn't even call me."

The murmurs from the room behind me stopped. If the whole world hadn't known about Tommy before, it did now.

"He wasn't accused of a crime, Ma. Don't you think I have enough on my mind right now without worrying about who knows what?"

"And even worse than anything," she

continued as though I hadn't said a word, "you were once again involved in a criminal investigation and didn't call me. I had to call you, remember? I mean, really. You find that Winters woman sprawled all over the band room, drenched in her own blood, and you didn't even see fit to let your own mother know. Why, I attended the garden club every month for years with Georgia's grandmother, not that you would recall. I've known her since before you were born. You know, one day I'll be dead and buried next to your father, and . . ."

She ranted on, but I wasn't listening. I had just remembered that my mother told me Georgia was thinking of selling the farm and April's last name was Winters. Was she a relation?

"Trish, are you listening to me?"

I looked up at my mother. She was standing directly in front of me. I hadn't even seen her move.

"Sorry, Ma." I needed to distract her. I leaned harder against the counter. "Being pregnant and all . . . I can't quite . . . well, I'm just so tired. . . ." I ended on a sigh, letting my words fade into the air. Inwardly, I smiled at my acting job. It's only fair that once in a while I turn the tables on the master manipulator, especially when it's to my benefit.

Her expression immediately changed to one of concern. "For heaven's sake! Why are you standing there? Go sit down. Are you trying to kill my newest grandchild before it's born?" She turned to April. "Make her a decaf latte with whole milk right now. I'll make a turkey club."

"But, Ma, I'm not hungry. I'm —"

"Don't argue with me, young lady." She pointed toward an empty table. "You're going to eat. Go sit down."

I ignored the surreptitious stares from everyone seated in the dining area and glanced at my watch as I obeyed my mother's orders. Fortunately, I had plenty of time to snack and still arrive at the high school early. I wanted to check out the band room.

Less than five minutes later, April delivered my sandwich and drink.

I waved at a chair. "Can you take a break for a couple of minutes?"

She glanced over at my mother, who was making an espresso for a local dentist. "Doris? You mind if I sit down with Trish?"

"I'd like the company," I whined for my mother's benefit as I tried to look drawn and weak. "It'll help me eat."

"Sure. Go on," Ma said. "It's time for

your break, anyway. Besides, it'll do Trish good."

I took a bite of my sandwich while April grabbed a cup of coffee and a chocolate biscotti. By the time she joined me, I had made a big dent in my sandwich.

She dropped into a chair across from me and smiled, then took a sip of coffee.

I wiped my mouth. "You wouldn't happen to be related to Georgia Winters, would you?"

April's smile died as if I'd slapped her. "Yes, I am. On my dad's side. The whole thing isn't a great topic with my family, and it's even worse right now."

I took a deep breath. "I don't want to be insensitive, but why?"

April rubbed her fingers on the coffee mug. "I'm really not sure. We think Granny Nettie is going senile. Georgia was taking care of her, but Granny was starting to need more care, like a home, so when Connie moved back, she started pitching in during the day while Georgia was at work. But then she started fighting with Georgia."

"Why?"

"Well, Georgia was getting tired. The farm was too much to take care of on top of everything else. She wanted to sell everything. But here's the rub. She wanted to

135

put Granny Nettie in a home. Connie didn't. She thought things should continue the way they were."

"So what's the relationship between Georgia, Connie, and Nettie? Why were they caring for her?"

"She's their aunt. Her husband died really young in some farming accident. They didn't have kids, so when Georgia and Connie were young, they spent every summer with her on the farm, and she just started treating them like her kids." April clicked her fingernail on the side of her coffee mug. "Things aren't good right now. And without Georgia, we're all sure Granny Nettie will have to go to a home. But Connie is insisting no. The bad thing is that Granny is losing things."

"Losing things? Like misplacing them?"

"That's what they say. It's that senile thing. She puts things places to keep them safe. Like, once she put her purse behind the ironing board in the laundry room. No one found it for days. But the really bad thing is that she's misplaced some valuable jewelry and knickknacks. Family heirlooms, I hear. The girls looked high and low for everything but found nothing."

"I'm sorry. That's horrible."

"Yeah. That's why Georgia wanted to put

Granny Nettie in a home and sell everything. Besides, she didn't want the responsibility anymore. And she wanted Connie to go back where she came from."

"Where was that?" I asked.

"Some town in Virginia. Charlotte something or other."

"So did Connie move here to help with Nettie?"

April shook her head. "Sort of. But she was also friends with that principal. You know? At the high school? I think she lived in that Charlotte place for a while, too."

A group of six construction workers walked through the front door.

"April!" Gail hollered. "We need you."

"Be there in a sec." April took a last sip of coffee and shoved the rest of the biscotti in her mouth.

"Thanks," I said.

"Your mom said you're going to solve this mystery." April stood and picked up her coffee cup. "I think you should. Even if it makes my family look bad. I feel really bad for Granny Nettie. I don't know what's going to happen to her now, but I'm glad I don't have to take care of her."

As she walked back behind the counter, I pulled my clue notebook from my purse. As I finished my sandwich, I studied the clues

I'd already written. Then I jotted down what April had told me.

Nettie treated Connie and Georgia like her own kids. Connie and Georgia fought about selling the farm and putting Nettie in a home. Georgia wanted to sell. Connie didn't. Nettie is losing her memory and losing things. (Is that important?)

I chewed the end of my pen. Money was a great motivation for murder. Had Connie killed her cousin? When she came to the self-storage facility the day before, she acted upset about Georgia's murder, but maybe that's all it was — an act. And Connie and Carla knew each other from . . . where was it? Was it Charlottesville? I made another note in my notebook.

A glance at my watch told me I'd better move on. I had a meeting to attend and more investigating to do.

Before I left, I convinced my mother to run a full-page ad in the play program. Really, all I had to do was tell her that the Cunninghams were doing the same. That's one area where my mother and I are in perfect agreement. The way we feel about Max's family.

I arrived a bit early for the play committee meeting, pausing for a deep breath at the band room door. My gaze slid around the room. To my relief, everything was in order.

"Marvin?" The baby was kicking my ribs and making it hard for me to breathe.

He didn't answer. The room was empty. I laid the boxes of doughnuts on a table and decided to take a quick look around before anyone arrived. I needed to see how the lock worked on the door in the instrument storage room that led out to the main hallway.

The storage room hadn't changed since I had been in the band. The various-sized wooden slots held instrument cases. There were only two high windows in the room. No way to escape through them. I walked over to the door that led from the room to the hall. When I had attended school here, the door was left open, and we could come and go as we pleased. Now a lock had been installed — a dead bolt that had to be unlocked with a key.

How did someone kill Georgia and escape from the room, leaving the only entrance to the band room blocked by a chair?

A sound behind me made me jump. I spun around, and Marvin was standing in the doorway to the storage room.

He took a step into the small room. "Mrs. Cunningham, what are you doing here?"

"Call me Trish, please," I said quickly.

I'd done just what I promised Max I wouldn't do. Put myself in a dangerous situation. How easy it would be for Marvin to bash me over the head with an instrument right now and leave me here, then claim he'd been somewhere else. Everyone would think we had a serial instrument basher at the school.

"Uh . . . I used to play the clarinet in marching band. I wondered if things had changed since then. They haven't." I pointed in the general direction of where I'd stored my instrument. "That's where my slot was."

He nodded. "Not a lot has changed around here at least in terms of the physical building. Lots of other things have changed, though."

His body language wasn't that of someone ready to attack me, so I relaxed a bit and motioned toward the door to the hall. "I guess that's one of the changes. We used to be able to come in and out of that door."

"That was done before I came. I keep it locked so that kids can't use the room to make out or steal instruments and pawn them."

"Pawn them?"

"Oh yeah," he said. "They use the money to buy drugs."

My little ideal world just kept crashing in

around me. Was I so naive?

He looked over his shoulder. "Say, did you bring the doughnuts?"

"Yes," I said. "Help yourself."

"I'm really hungry." He turned and walked back into the band room.

I took a deep breath of relief, but I could see that keeping my promise to Max to stay out of danger while I gathered clues was going to be harder than I thought.

By the time I walked out of the storage room, Marvin was stuffing his face with a doughnut as if he hadn't eaten in a week. With powdered sugar on his lips, his dress shirt hanging limply on broad, bony shoulders, and pants resting low on his narrow hips, he looked a bit like a scarecrow.

Carla strode into the room and greeted me with a nod and Marvin with a cool glance. She had a clipboard in her hands with papers half an inch thick piled on it. I guessed Max had already talked with her, but she gave me no indication either way, just acknowledged me with that slight nod. I had a feeling she had difficulty focusing on more than one thing at a time. What I didn't understand was why the principal of the school was so involved in the play. Didn't she have office things to do?

When she noticed the boxes I'd brought,

she put the clipboard down and chose a cake doughnut, which she delicately nibbled, dabbing her lips with her napkin after each bite.

Other people arrived, including a woman who looked so much like Detective Scott, I knew she had to be his sister. She headed straight for me. That's when I noticed she walked with a cane and a decided limp.

"You've got to be Trish Cunningham," she said when she reached me. "I'm Elissa Scott."

She held out her hand, which I automatically clasped. Her grip was firm and strong. She was tall, with gray eyes and an assessing gaze. I wondered why she was here.

"I'm glad to meet you. I heard you were living with Detective Scott."

"Ah yes." She glanced around at the people gathering in the room then back at me. "News does fly around here."

"Yep." I grinned. "But I also know your niece."

She smiled. "She speaks highly of you and your family."

"She might like me, but I'm not sure your brother does."

Elissa laughed. "Don't worry about him. If he didn't like you, you'd know for sure." Her gaze swept over me. "So, when is your baby due?"

"Less than a month."

"All right, ladies and gentlemen, we need to start this meeting." Carla slapped her clipboard down on Marvin's music stand, interrupting my conversation with Elissa. Marvin's baton fell to the floor, and anger flashed in his eyes as he bent over to pick it up. I was trying to figure out the dynamics between him and Carla when, from the side of my eye, I saw motion at the band room door and turned to see Sherry waving wildly through the window.

I nudged Elissa with my arm. "Does Sherry want me or you?"

Elissa looked over at her niece, who was now pointing with thrusts of her index finger in our direction. "You, I think."

"Excuse me," I murmured. I crossed the room and opened the door. "What's up?"

"Mrs. C., I have to talk to you." The tone of her voice was low and urgent.

"Trish?" Carla said behind me. "We must start this meeting now."

I glanced around and realized that everyone was seated and staring at me. I turned back to Sherry. "All right, why don't you call my cell phone in about an hour?"

"You don't understand," she said. "My dad is on a rampage."

Her anxiety was catching, and my stomach clenched, but I needed to be cool. "I'm not surprised. He's rampaged before."

"No." The poor child was wringing her hands. "Not like this."

"Trish?" Carla repeated in her bossy tone.

"I have to get back to the meeting. I'll call you when I'm done." I patted Sherry's arm. "Don't worry. Things will be fine." I was trying to assure her even though I didn't believe it myself.

Her shoulders slumped. "Just be prepared, okay?" She turned and walked slowly down the hall, leaving me feeling anxious.

I tried to ignore the dread that settled in my stomach as I shut the door. Elissa saved me a seat next to her and patted it. She'd hung her cane on the back of her chair.

"What's up?" she whispered.

"She says her dad is on a rampage."

Elissa snorted, which relieved some of my tension. I had a feeling I was going to like her, but she didn't have a chance to say anything, because Carla glanced at us and pointedly cleared her throat.

"I have drawn up a tentative schedule of when everyone's tasks should be completed." She motioned imperiously at Marvin. "Please hand this out." Then she frowned and looked around the room.

"Where is Connie? Marvin, do you know?"

"No, I don't," he said in a flat tone without looking at her. He continued passing out papers as Carla had ordered.

"Well, that's . . ." Carla took a breath. "Well, we'll just work around her, then. You." She pointed at Elissa. "You said you wanted to help somehow. You can help Connie with costumes. You'll need to get in touch with her."

She turned to me. "Now, Trish, please tell us whom you have approached for advertising."

I pulled a folded piece of paper from my purse. It wasn't really a list — I was just pretending — but I didn't need a reminder of the two whole people I'd already talked to. I would just do some quick faking for the rest.

I had opened my mouth to begin my recitation when the door flew open and Detective Eric Scott strode into the room.

Everyone stared at him. I thought Carla was going to have a stroke.

"We're having a meeting here," she said.

"Excuse me. Sheriff's office business." He scanned the room, his gaze skimming over his sister, then locking with mine.

"Trish," he said. "I'd like a word with you. Will you please come with me?"

9

Detective Scott motioned for me to go ahead of him and pulled the band room door shut.

"Why do you do things like this?" I demanded. "Everyone's going to think I killed Georgia or something."

He pointed up the hall as if I hadn't spoken, which didn't surprise me. "Let's go outside to my car."

I stopped midstep. "Can't we talk here? I don't feel like going outside. I need to be in that meeting." The truth was I couldn't have cared less about the meeting, but I was in no mood to talk to him. Sherry had correctly called it. Her father was on a rampage, although it wouldn't be apparent to the casual observer. Self-controlled types like Detective Scott and Max, and even my father, show their emotions in subtle ways, like clenched jaws, stiff bodies, and deceptively low-pitched voices. Not in loud outbursts like my mother. Subtlety was much more intimidating to me.

"We're going outside," he said in a flat tone.

I met his intimidating gaze and shrugged. I would go with him because he was an officer of the law. He had the badge and the gun. However, I would not let myself be browbeaten.

"I've been thinking about all of this," I said breathlessly as I tried to keep pace with him. "Because of that chair behind the door to the band room, there's no way anyone could have left after they bashed in Georgia's head . . . unless they went through the door in the instrument storage room. The door to the instrument room is locked with a dead bolt that you need a key to unlock. Who all has keys? I imagine Marvin does. So would Carla. Actually, so would anybody who had school access. Keys can be copied."

He grunted.

"I wish you would slow down," I grumbled. "I can't breathe."

He did, just a smidgeon.

"This way," he said when we reached the front doors.

He held one open for me, and I walked through. My thoughts were gaining momentum. "Really, now that I think about it, I can't be sure Georgia was bashed with the bassoon. I didn't look at it closely, but I should have. It seems to me there should have been more blood all over the place."

He was walking more quickly now, ahead of me. I trailed behind him, down the sidewalk to his car. When he got there, he turned and faced me with crossed arms.

"What?" I was trying to catch my breath. The baby was kicking my ribs and pressing up against my lungs. "So? Was she bashed with the bassoon?"

"You know I can't give you details."

"Well, you should. I'm not my mother. I'm trustworthy. I could help you." The look in his eyes would have frozen most people to death, but not me. I was too keyed up now to be immobilized by the likes of a rampaging detective. "So what do you want, anyway?"

He looked down at me. "You're investigating the attack on Georgia Winters even though I told you not to."

"Max knows. I told him. Besides, I'm just checking up on things and writing down notes." I stretched my back muscles, which felt like massive, twisted rubber bands.

"Like my daughter is checking up on things?" He said the words so softly, I almost missed them.

Suddenly everything was clear. Detective Scott's rampaging. Sherry's fear. She'd been caught, and she was probably in trouble.

Oh, who was I kidding? *I* was in trouble. I wondered how he'd found out she was looking into things. Then I realized that was stupid. He was a master interrogator. He probably tortured her with his tapping pen.

I met his scowl with crossed arms, mirroring his stubborn stance. "Writing down notes won't hurt anybody."

A satisfied gleam filled his eyes. "So you knew what she was doing?"

"I didn't say that." When would I ever learn to keep my mouth shut? "And writing things down isn't dangerous," I reiterated.

"That depends on how the information is obtained. And it sometimes shows a decided lack of good judgment, especially when people are dabbling where they shouldn't."

"So why don't you tell me exactly how you feel?" I snapped. "Like you don't think I have good judgment?"

He took a deep breath. "Listen, my daughter is stubborn —"

My snort of laughter stopped him.

"What do you find so amusing?" he asked. "There is nothing funny at all about this situation."

"Well, yeah, there is. It's *you* saying *Sherry*

is stubborn. Did you expect something different? She's *your* daughter. That alone is enough, really, but come on, Detective. She's also a teenager. And teenager is synonymous with stubborn."

"What do you mean she's my . . ." He shook his head and took a deep breath. "Her age has nothing to do with this. Poor judgment is poor judgment." His eyes flashed.

"So both of us have poor judgment?"

"You said it, not me," he growled.

Poor Sherry — having to deal with him on a regular basis. If only Abbie knew how badly they needed a steadying influence.

"I need to ask you about her, Tommy, and this —"

"Her and Tommy?" I narrowed my eyes at him. "Is that why you're so snippy? Because of Tommy and your daughter? And what about Tommy, Detective Scott? Is he a suspect? Because this whole thing is ruining his reputation. Today my mother informed everyone within fifty miles that you'd questioned him. Not that I should be surprised about that. She has a big mouth. But I really need to know. Is Tommy a suspect?"

The emotion in the detective's eyes died, and his expression flattened. "You know I'm not going to discuss that."

Now I was starting to lose my temper, and, unfortunately, I couldn't control myself nearly as well as he could. "Tommy is my son!"

"And he's almost eighteen," Detective Scott said.

We stared at each other, both of us breathing hard.

"Well, your daughter *is* eighteen. She's officially an adult, so she can do what she likes." I dropped my arms and frowned at him. "And Tommy isn't guilty. How could he be? Even your daughter likes him. That has to mean something."

"Sherry is still immature and doesn't have good sense —"

He snapped his jaw shut. He must have seen the look in my eyes.

We glared at each other. A true standoff. He gave in first.

"I'm sorry. This isn't personal. Or it shouldn't be. Tommy hasn't been charged with anything. But I'm not going to discuss that any further with you."

"I consider your attitude very personal." I wanted to stomp on his toes, but that would be considered assaulting a police officer. I backed up a step. "Are we done?"

"No," the detective said. "I want to know who you've been talking to."

I stared up at him. "Besides Abbie, you mean?"

Touché. He stared at me like a dog with a new food dish.

I tried not to smile with satisfaction. "I'm sure that whole experience put you in a bad mood, but just because she's my best friend doesn't mean you have to take it out on me and Tommy. Besides, why should I tell you anything I find out? You won't tell me anything." Even as I said the words, I knew how immature I sounded. Anger had a way of doing that to me.

His fingers twitched, and he inhaled several times. "I can arrest you for obstruction."

"I doubt that," I said. "I watch television. I'm not obstructing anything. You have no proof I even know anything that would help you with the case. In fact, you're obstructing me. You pulled me out of a meeting and —"

I heard footsteps. The detective's gaze flickered over my shoulder.

"Hey there, Mrs. C. You feelin' okay?" Corporal Fletcher's voice boomed at us.

I turned my back to Detective Scott and faced the corporal. "No. I'm *not* okay."

Behind me I heard Detective Scott's ragged sigh. "Great timing, Fletcher."

Corporal Fletcher's round face drooped. "Sorry, Sarge. Did I interrupt?"

"Yes," Detective Scott said.

"No," I said.

Corporal Fletcher's eyes widened, and his bushy brows rose nearly to his hairline.

"I'm not done talking to you," Detective Scott said.

"Well, I'm done talking to you." I was too mad to even pray and ask God to help me get rid of my anger.

"Trish," Detective Scott said. "If you insist on investigating, be careful."

He sounded so worried I wanted to cave in, but I didn't. No way would I share my notes *or* my best friend with someone who thought my son was a criminal and a bad influence.

I was walking past Corporal Fletcher who looked as worried as the detective sounded.

"Mrs. C., we mean it," the corporal said. He glanced over my head at Detective Scott in some sort of unspoken communication. "Maybe you could even avoid, er, socializing at the school for a while."

As I walked away, I wondered what that meant, but I wouldn't lower myself to turn around and ask.

On my way home, I talked to Sherry on the

phone, and she apologized for her father's actions. She sounded as if she were about to cry, so I didn't tell her how mad I really was — at her and her father. I didn't like being stuck between the two of them. When I tried once more to talk her out of investigating, she just argued with me. Truthfully, I could understand Detective Scott's frustration with her, and I ended the conversation a little abruptly, ignoring her hurt tone.

Max's car was in the driveway when I got home. I was still steaming mad and ready to dump everything on my husband. I wanted him to sic one of his flashy lawyer friends on Detective Sergeant Eric Scott the know-it-all.

I slammed the door between the kitchen and the garage and flung my purse down on the kitchen table. "Max?" I yelled.

No answer. I stalked down the hall to the front of the house where his office was. The door was shut.

"Max?" I grabbed the knob and pushed. *Locked.*

After a stunned moment, I pressed my ear against the door. I heard murmurs from inside. He was on the phone. My temper, which was already in high gear, roared into overdrive. I wanted to pound the door with my fists, but instead, I took a deep breath and waited.

The murmuring stopped, and then I heard the sounds of Max's shoes on the wood floor. The lock clicked, and he opened the door.

"Why did you lock me out?" I demanded.

"Because I didn't want to be interrupted." Max looked even more tired than he had that morning.

"What's wrong? Did the talk go badly with Carla? Is Tommy going to be expelled or something?"

"The cheating isn't going to be a problem. She knows he didn't do that." He put his hands on my shoulders and turned me around. "Let's go to the kitchen. I could use a glass of lemonade before I go back to work."

"But —" I stopped. "You're going back to work? Why?"

"Because I have to." Max gently prodded me down the hall.

"What if I wanted to spend time with you? I hardly ever see you anymore."

"We're both pretty busy," Max said as we walked into the kitchen.

"Well, do you have time to talk right now?"

"A few minutes," he said.

I bit back a sarcastic comment about making an appointment in the future. "Well, you wouldn't believe what happened today."

"What?" Max murmured as he pulled open the refrigerator and pulled out the pitcher of lemonade. "Want some?"

"Yes, please." I crossed my arms. "Sherry is insisting on investigating Georgia's murder. To save Tommy. And now Detective Scott is mad at me."

Max set the pitcher on the counter and turned to face me. "Sherry is investigating? Because of Tommy? You knew this?"

I nodded. "Yes. And what choice did I have? Last night she told me she wanted the two of us to investigate together. I told her no. She argued and said she'd do it without me if I wouldn't agree to work with her."

Max frowned at me as if it were all my fault.

"Stop looking at me like that." I dropped into a chair and waved my hand. "What was I supposed to do? I know she'd do it on her own anyway. She's stubborn."

His green eyes narrowed. "I guess you would know."

"That's not nice."

"Well, maybe you should have told Eric. Wouldn't you have wanted someone to tell us if it were one of our kids?"

Max had a point, and I didn't like it. "I

guess I was just burying my head in the sand. But Detective Scott found out today and yelled at me."

"Did you get it straightened out?" Max pulled two glasses from the cupboard.

"Not really," I said. "I, uh, sort of yelled back at him."

Max glanced at me over his shoulder. "You yelled at him? That probably wasn't real sm— Um, productive."

Max had almost said "smart." That hurt me. "Detective Scott deserved it. He insinuated that Tommy was guilty and that he didn't want Sherry involved with him."

Max poured the lemonade and handed me a glass. "Are you sure you didn't misunderstand him?"

"Well, it's possible," I said grudgingly and slouched in the chair and took a sip as I considered how I felt. "It's really possible. I'm afraid, Max, and my fear could be coloring everything. I don't like the way things are going right now. Not with the kids involved."

"Yeah, me, too." He leaned back against the counter.

"Do you think they're safe at school?"

He hesitated before he answered. "I want to think so."

"Did you know that Karen wanted to

157

investigate, too?"

Max put his glass down hard on the counter. "This keeps getting worse. I hope you told her no."

"Of course I did, but I can't stop what they do at school. And Detective Scott keeps questioning me."

Max stared at me. "I don't think Eric seriously believes that Tommy murdered Georgia."

"Well then, why won't he leave us alone?" I asked.

"He's doing his job, that's all. And I suspect he's making sure you tell him everything you saw that's relevant. The faster he gets this crime solved, the faster some things get back to normal."

Max turned around and stared out the window above the sink. Something else was bugging him. Could today's conversation behind a locked door have anything to do with what he had hidden from me on his desk at work? He took a deep breath then picked up the pitcher.

"Max, what's wrong?"

His fingers tightened on the handle of the pitcher as he put it in the refrigerator. "That's a silly question."

"Well, you act like you're keeping secrets from me," I said. "Remember when Jim Bob was murdered? We agreed. No more secrets. I kept my word. I told you when I was keeping notes. Today you had your office door locked. You were also shoving something around on your desk at work yesterday. What was that about?"

Max took a deep breath. Then he turned to face me. "I have a lot of things on my mind right now and —"

The door to the garage flew open and banged against the wall. Karen burst into the kitchen, followed by Sherry.

"Tommy is at the sheriff's office," Karen said.

"What?" Max and I said at the same time.

Sherry started crying. "My dad took Tommy in for questioning. This is all my fault."

10

Max knows lawyers with Harvard educations because he went to Harvard, and he takes full advantage of their services when he needs them. I was familiar with the man he hired to represent Tommy. Calvin Schiller had represented me during the investigation into Jim Bob Jensen's murder months ago.

I hadn't liked Calvin's attitude back then, and it hadn't changed. When we arrived at the sheriff's office, he was waiting for us in the lobby. He glanced at me as if I were a wad of gum stuck on the bottom of his shoe. Then he smiled at Max.

"Everything is fine," he said in his newscaster quality voice. "They can't question him until I get to the interview room. It'll be short and sweet, believe me." I imagined Calvin came across well in court. His gray suit hung on his portly body with the perfection one can buy only from a personal tailor. He looked to be the perfect combination of sophistication and aged wisdom.

"Should we go with you?" I asked. "I'd really like to be there."

Calvin lost his self-possession for a moment and looked horrified. "No," he said quickly. "I'll take care of everything."

I glanced at Max and read his thoughts. I should butt out.

I tamped down my protective nature while the two of them talked in hushed tones. Max had relaxed. I guessed everything would be fine. Calvin might be a snob, but he was a smart snob. If he said things were okay, I believed him. I told Max I'd meet him outside; then I went out to the SUV. I had some thoughts to put in my notebook.

As I walked to the vehicle, I pulled out my phone. Before I could do anything else, I had to console Sherry, who had begged me to call her with any news.

She answered on the first half of the first ring. "Mrs. C., is Tommy okay?"

"The lawyer is here and assures us things are fine." I unlocked the doors to the SUV and plopped into the passenger seat and shut the door.

Her rapid breaths hissed through the speaker. "Well, this is my fault."

I was relieved she thought so. She should leave the investigation in more capable hands. Like mine and her father's.

"So you'll stop sleuthing, right?" I asked. "Stop asking questions?"

"No way," she said.

I was momentarily speechless, which was just as well, because she obviously had more to tell me.

"I have to keep going on this. I'm in a great position to hear things at the school. Like I said, no one pays much attention to me. I can find out stuff even you can't. I've already learned a couple of interesting things."

As much as I wanted to know the interesting things she'd found out, I was more afraid of her father's reaction. "Sherry, you, uh, said Tommy being hauled down here was your fault for investigating. What did you have in your notebook?"

"Not much. Just a few things. But enough that Daddy knew what I was doing."

"But if your investigating got Tommy in trouble, shouldn't you stop before something else happens?"

She laughed — just a little maniacally, I thought. "Oh, I didn't mean it was because I investigated. It was my fault because I was stupid enough to leave my notebook where Daddy could find it."

Her statement was illogically logical.

Shades of me. That was scary.

"I don't know about this —"

"Don't worry, Mrs. C. I'll be fine."

"Your father is frantic with worry. I understand how he feels."

I felt anger in her silence.

"Sherry —"

"Does that mean you don't want to hear what I've found out?"

"If I can't talk you out of investigating, will you promise me something?"

"What?" she asked.

"Keep your cell phone with you at all times. Don't put yourself in any dangerous situations. Make sure your dad knows where you are."

"I will. I promise."

She had agreed too quickly, and her promise was about as useless as mine was to Max. Sometimes dangerous situations just happen. I had to think of a way to get her to stop, but in the meantime, I did want to know what she had discovered.

"All right. Tell me what you learned."

"I volunteer in the library sometimes, and the librarians are always gossiping. They think Mr. Slade likes the costume lady."

"Connie Gilbert?"

"Yeah. And Ms. Winters and Ms. Gilbert, the costume lady, had a huge fight the day

Ms. Winters was murdered. In the library. Ms. Gilbert was in there using the computer."

"The librarian said something about an argument."

"Well, Ms. Winters made Ms. Gilbert get off the computer and leave the library."

"Do you know why?"

"Nope, but they were both really mad. I wonder if there was some sort of love triangle going on between Ms. Winters, Mr. Slade, and Ms. Gilbert." Sherry's breath came faster. "Maybe Mr. Slade and Ms. Gilbert were . . . you know."

I didn't want Sherry to be thinking about things like . . . you know. Especially since she was interested in my son.

"Maybe that's why Ms. Winters is dead," Sherry said.

Love triangles. That meant potential hostility. Lots of it. "This is really serious. You shouldn't —"

"And Ms. Bickford has a plan," she announced.

"A plan? What kind of a plan?"

"I don't know. I overheard that when I was in the library, too. You should have heard that librarian." Sherry giggled. "She hates cops and was bragging that she was questioned and didn't give in. I don't think she knows who my dad is."

"I can guarantee she doesn't know who your dad is, or you wouldn't be in there helping her." I questioned Sherry for more details about Carla, but she had none.

"There's an emergency closed-door school board meeting tonight," she said. "Oh, and one more thing."

"What's that?"

"This is really strange. My dad told me not to eat or drink anything that anyone gives me. Only what I bring to school myself."

"Why?" I remembered what Corporal Fletcher had said about socializing at the school.

"He wouldn't say, but I already told Tommy."

That changed things. The danger wasn't hypothetical anymore; it was very real.

"Sherry . . ." I wanted to try to stop her from investigating further.

"Don't say it, Mrs. C. You can't talk me out of it. So I'll call you if I find out anything else." Then she hung up.

I pushed the END button on my cell phone. Sherry was right. She *could* find out things that no one else could. However, the more I learned, the more concerned I was.

Max made a good point earlier. I would

want to know if one of my kids was behaving like Sherry. As much as I dreaded doing it, I had to let Detective Scott know she was pursuing her investigation.

In the meantime, I needed to add to my notes. I got my clue notebook and awkwardly balanced it on the purse on my knees. I added, *Connie and Georgia had a big fight in the library. Georgia made Connie get off the computer. Possible love triangle between Georgia, Marvin, and Connie. Carla has a plan.*

Detective Scott told Sherry not to eat or drink at the school.

I paused to reflect on that point. Did that mean that Georgia hadn't been bashed in the head? Maybe she'd been poisoned? I tapped my pen furiously on the paper, rereading everything I'd written.

I was flipping through my pages when a tap on the window made me jump. I looked up and saw Corporal Fletcher standing there in his uniform.

"Hey," I said, after I rolled down the window.

"Hi, Mrs. C. You okay?"

"Yep."

He looked at the notebook in my hand then back up at me with a sharpened gaze. "Keeping notes?"

I slapped the notebook shut. "Yes. Now perhaps you can tell me why I should avoid socializing at the school."

He cleared his throat and wouldn't meet my eyes. "Just trust me, Mrs. C."

"You mean, like don't ingest anything anyone gives me?"

"Um, yeah."

The way the cops had to pussyfoot around irritated me.

After glancing over the top of my SUV, he rubbed his shoe on the pavement then met my gaze. "Listen, Sarge is a good guy, really."

"Well, you couldn't prove it by me," I said irritably.

"He's worried and under a great deal of pressure to solve this case." Corporal Fletcher sighed. "I shouldn't talk about this, but he, um, really likes your friend."

"Really? Well that's too bad. I wouldn't wish him on anyone."

"Come on, Mrs. C. That's a little harsh."

"Well, he was really rude to me today."

"He's worried about you and about Sherry."

"Then he should say that instead of acting like a jerk."

The corporal shook his head. "You know what our jobs are like. We aren't trained to

167

be sweethearts."

"Maybe not, but I still don't like it."

"Listen, you only see his cop side. Really, he's a great guy." Corporal Fletcher was so earnest.

"Abbie thinks he's going to get even with her for turning him down. Like not helping her research her books anymore."

"That's not like him at all."

"Well, after we had our *discussion* this afternoon, and he found out I knew about Abbie, he immediately went and pulled Tommy in for questioning."

The corporal shook his head. "One had nothing to do with the other." He leaned toward me. "He wouldn't hurt her. He likes her a lot." He eyed me with one slightly raised brow.

I met his gaze, and the truth finally dawned on me. "You want us to play matchmaker, don't you? I can't believe you. No. I don't think so, Corporal Fletcher. You don't know Abbie. She's —"

He put his arms behind his back and stared at me with no expression.

"Oh yeah," I said. "Go hide behind your blank cop look. I'm a mother. I can read minds."

The corner of his mouth twitched. "He makes good money. He owns his own house.

He's stable." He winked at me. "He thinks your friend is a knockout."

"He thinks Abbie is . . . well, I have to agree. I'm glad he noticed, because she is. But, really. He has an angry daughter. He's annoyingly persistent. He carries a gun, and he has irregular hours."

"Mmm," was all Corporal Fletcher said.

"Mmm," I imitated him. "I hate it when you guys *mmm*." Then a sudden thought crossed my mind. "Did Detective Scott request to be Abbie's consultant?"

For a moment, I didn't think Corporal Fletcher would answer. Then he nodded.

Perhaps the corporal was right. If Detective Scott wanted to see Abbie that badly, she should at least go out with him. Maybe he would be nicer to me if he was dating her.

"So?" Corporal Fletcher asked.

"Oh, okay. Fine. I'll give it some thought." I eyed him. "So, while you're being so friendly and all, how close are you to solving the murder?"

The amused look in his eyes died. "It's an ongoing investigation."

"I know, but why would someone kill Georgia?"

Corporal Fletcher stood taller and put his hands to his side. "Mrs. C., you know better. I can't talk about that."

"Not even just saying yes or no? Like, if I ask a question, you could just nod or shake your head?"

"Not even," he said.

"Figures," I grumbled. "Well, I'm keeping my ears open, anyway."

He leaned forward and put his hands on the car. "What have you heard?"

"Is that fair?" I said to the corporal. "You won't tell me anything, but you expect me to share?"

"You should tell us anything you know that could be useful," he droned.

I shrugged. "I have very little information, but I plan to talk to some other people." I took a deep breath. "Sherry is still insisting on asking questions, too, even though her father told her not to." I felt like a traitor.

"That young lady has real issues." The corporal leaned against my SUV. "You know I should tell Sarge she's still up to that."

"I agree. Better you tell him than me. You know, Corporal Fletcher, I *am* a mom, and despite how irresponsible Detective Scott thinks I am, I don't want anyone's kid in danger."

"He doesn't think that, and neither do I."

"Earlier today he implied I lacked good judgment."

"He was just frustrated. Really, we just think you're . . ." He stuck his thumb in his belt. "Well, we think you're overzealous."

I had to smile at that. "That's a nice way to say that I'm terribly annoying. All right. I'll let you know if I find out anything important."

The front door of the building opened, and Max and Calvin Schiller strode out onto the sidewalk and headed toward the parking lot.

Corporal Fletcher straightened, a frown etching deep lines in his forehead. "You investigating this is not a good idea, Mrs. C."

"Why not?" I asked.

"I don't have to tell you that. You know exactly what can happen when a murderer gets mad."

11

When I walked into the self-storage office on Thursday morning, Shirl greeted me with a toothpaste commercial smile. Stranger still, I saw books on her desk that weren't her usual bodice-ripping fare. But the oddest thing of all was the lineup of assorted sizes of bottles and plastic bags filled with dried green and brown weedy-looking stuff.

"Hope the cops don't come by. It looks like you're dealing drugs." I grabbed the mail. "I assume these are legal?"

She sniffed and waved her arm over the assembled plastic containers. "These are herbs." She pronounced the *h.* "They're going to keep me from having to ever use pharmaceutical drugs again."

Pharmaceutical. That was a big word. I glanced over her collection and wondered if one of them was black *cobash.*

She tapped the stack of books. "I'm studying these now. That's where I've been going at lunch. To classes. My pharmacist teaches them."

"Oh." I thumbed through the envelopes looking for bills to pay.

She narrowed her eyes and stared at me. "You really do look like you could use something. You're pale and puffy, and you look tense. There's herbs for that, too, you know."

"Puffy?" I looked at my fingers. "I'm puffy?"

She looked me up and down. "Your ankles maybe. It could just be all the weight you've gained, but you're probably holding water, too."

"All the weight I've gained? My ankles are puffy?" I knew my pants were tight, but . . .

Shirl stared pointedly at my hips. "Well, it's to be expected. Mr. C. said you're eating like three times as much as normal."

"He said that?"

Before Shirl could answer, she was distracted by someone outside. "Now who is that, I wonder?"

I didn't care. I had my leg extended so I could stare at my ankle. It did look swollen. I had to call Max right away and ask him if he thought I was fat. Was that why he was avoiding me lately?

Shirl squinted. "That guy out there sure looks familiar, but he hasn't been here before, I know that. I know all of our customers by sight and name."

Finally, I turned and peered through the large front window at the man getting out of his car. I would have recognized his lanky frame anywhere.

"It's Marvin Slade," I said to Shirl.

"Marvin Slade?" Shirl stood and leaned over the counter to stare at him as he walked up the sidewalk to the front door. "Name sounds familiar."

"It should. He's the band director at the high school."

Shirl harrumphed. "One of the suspects, you mean."

Marvin met my gaze through the glass as he grabbed the doorknob.

Shirl was breathing hard. "We need to get him out of here as quickly as possible, Mrs. C. We don't need murderers coming . . ."

"Hi, Marvin," I said over her voice. "What can we do for you?"

"I'm just here to check something in Connie's new storage unit. Costume stuff." He pulled a shiny key from his pocket. "I have the key and the code to get through the gate. Is it okay for me to go in there?"

"As long as you have the key and the code,

you can go into the unit."

Shirl made noises behind me, opening a file drawer and slamming it, but I ignored her.

"Is Connie okay?" I asked.

He shrugged. "How should I know?"

"Well, that's what I thought," Shirl said.

We both turned toward her.

She waved a contract in my face. "Connie's got Georgia down as her emergency contact, not Marvin."

He swallowed and turned his watery gaze on me.

I felt sorry for him and wanted to agree with what my daughter had said. This man couldn't possibly be a murderer. Still, some of the worst killers in history looked and acted harmless in public.

"What does that mean?" he asked. "I can't go in?"

Shirl sniffed. "Well —"

"It's fine," I said to Shirl. "You know the rules. When someone has the key, they can go in. Besides, I'm part of all this, too, because of the play." I turned to him. "You can go in. You've got my permission."

Marvin's wide, bony shoulders were hunched over as if he were in pain. He looked like a hound dog someone had hit with salt pellets from a shotgun. He smiled weakly at me. "I don't know where her units are."

"I'll show you." I motioned to the door. "I'll walk up there. Once you get through the gate, you can follow me in your car."

As I walked behind him to the front door, I heard Shirl clear her throat.

"Now I know where I saw you," she blurted out. "At the pharmacy. Night before last, around seven."

Marvin turned and eyed her over my shoulder as though she were a stalker. I didn't blame him.

"Shirl has a memory for faces," I explained. "That's why she's so good at her job here." I didn't bother to tell him she could rival my mother for collecting gossip and facts about people.

"Oh." He still looked at her with drawn brows. "Well, I'll be going then." He edged toward the door.

"You be careful," Shirl said. "What with your heart and all, we wouldn't want you to keel over dead in the parking lot."

My mouth dropped open, probably in a good imitation of Marvin's. Whatever herbs Shirl was taking seemed to have short-circuited what little control she normally had on her mouth. I had my back to her, so when Marvin glanced at me with wide eyes,

I rolled mine toward the ceiling and mouthed, "I'm sorry."

He dipped his head in acknowledgment, turned, and left without further comment.

"He's a weirdo," Shirl said behind me.

It takes one to know one, as my mother would say.

I faced her. "How do you know he has a heart problem?"

"I heard him talking to my new pharmacist about some kind of heart medicine."

"And you just stood there and listened?"

She shrugged. "Can't help but overhear things, the place is so small."

"Well, why is he a weirdo?"

"He's known as a ladies' man. Now that I've seen him, I'm shocked. Can you believe it, the way he looks with that bald head and elf ears? I heard he's always dating someone." Shirl shook her head. "Makes you wonder what he's got going for himself. Can you imagine?"

No, I couldn't. Nor did I want to.

"I'm going to show him where Connie's unit is." I twisted the knob on the front door.

"If you're not back in five minutes, I'm calling the cops and coming up there with a baseball bat. I keep one in my car, you know." Shirl opened a large tote bag and began stuffing her various bottles and bags into its depths. "You shouldn't be alone with a murderer."

"We don't know he's a murderer."

"And we don't know he isn't. I'll tell you what. There's just something not right about a man like that. Ugly as a catfish but gets women. You mind my words. It's a black widower thing. Some kind of attraction that normal women can't feel, but the victims . . . they're needy."

"Shirl!"

"You know it's true. Now, if he looked like Mr. C., I could understand it. I mean all the women swoon over him. He's as nice as he is good-looking. You should hear what they say when he walks away, especially about his . . ." She glanced quickly at me then away again. "Well, anyway, he just gets better looking as time goes by. I'm surprised you don't have to put a ball and chain on him to keep him from wandering."

Just what I needed to hear when I was already feeling fat and undesirable. Unwelcome feelings of insecurity crammed my mind with pictures of model-like women swarming all over my husband. And me with my tight maternity pants, fat behind, and swollen ankles. Why hadn't I noticed I was gaining that much weight? I had to get away from Shirl because I had a sudden urge to cry.

I met Marvin at the entrance to the climate-controlled building and showed him how to use the code. We stepped inside, and I pointed to Connie's units, keeping a good five feet between us. I intended to question him, and if he made a move toward me, I would be able to escape. My first goal was to determine which of the two women he had been interested in.

"I'm really sorry about your loss," I said.

His forehead wrinkled in a frown. "My loss?"

"Um, yeah. Georgia?" I backed up a few steps toward the door, getting ready to run if I had to.

He blinked. "Why would I care about her? All she did was make people's lives miserable. Well, at least Connie's."

He sounded angry. I pressed my body against the door. "Have you seen Connie lately?"

"Yes," he said. "Why do you want to know?"

I shrugged. "Just wondered. So, are you on your break or lunch or something?"

"Break?" he asked.

"Yeah. I'm surprised you aren't at school today."

His eyes flashed with annoyance. "Yeah, a break."

This wasn't going to be productive at all, and he was making me nervous.

Suddenly, his eyes met mine, and his face darkened with anger. "I know what you're doing."

"You do?"

"You're trying to solve this mystery, aren't you? I've heard about you."

I stepped backward toward the door until I felt it against my back.

"I didn't kill her," he said.

I groped behind me for the door handle. "Um, that's great. I'm glad. You could go to jail for that. And be executed . . . and all." Shirl's words about him being a murderer kept ringing in my head. "Do you need anything else?"

He shook his head. "No, nothing. I'm fine. Thank you."

I yanked the door open, rushed down the parking lot, and flung open the door to the office.

Shirl looked up from her computer. "Well? Did he try to kill you?

"Would I be standing here if he had?" I giggled, but it was from nervousness. "In fact, he assured me he hadn't killed her."

Shirl snorted. "Mark my words. Something's up with him."

I walked back to my office and fired up my computer, trying to quell the shakiness in my knees. After checking through some e-mails and opening the bills, I had calmed down enough to think logically. Maybe I should look over my notes. I needed to start thinking of intelligent questions to find the answers to.

A big one: *Motive. What reason would the suspects who had access to Georgia have to murder her?*

I looked at my suspect list. I had to find out more about everyone. Including Georgia. But I could jot down a few ideas.

Marvin Slade — pawning instruments? He had a key. He was there.

Carla Bickford — has a plan. What plan — is it what she mentioned about upping the school security system?

Connie Gilbert — angry with Georgia? Why? Fighting over selling the farm?

Coach Kent Smith — giving kids steroids? Didn't want Jason kicked off the team?

No other suspects made sense.

"That Marvin person is leaving," Shirl yelled from the other office. "Now what do you suppose he was doing? Hiding a murder weapon?"

"I doubt it," I yelled back. I didn't tell her my suspicions.

I jotted down, *How: Was she murdered with the bassoon, or was it poison?*

I needed to find out more about the people involved in this, and I knew one person who had access to information from all over town.

I called Doris's Doughnuts, and my mother answered. She must have seen my name on caller ID. "Trish, I hope this isn't bad news. I've been worried sick about you. Just sick."

I felt guilty for leading her on the day before. "I'm fine, Ma. I just have a question for you."

"Are you sure you're fine? You should go to the doctor."

"I am. Tomorrow. Listen, I need to know everything you know about Georgia, Marvin Slade, Connie Gilbert, Carla Bickford, and Kent Smith."

"Well, hallelujah and pass the offering plate. You *are* solving this mystery." I heard her hand rubbing on the receiver as she covered it. "Girls," she yelled. "You wouldn't believe it, but Trish is going to solve this mystery."

"Ma, please. Don't advertise the fact."

She laughed. "Nobody here is going to tell anyone."

Right. And doughnuts are fat free.

"I'll do some asking around." She sounded excited.

"That would be great. And you're watching Charlie and Sammie tonight so I can go to Bible study, right?"

"Yes," she said.

Maybe this would put me back in her good graces for a while. I hung up and tucked my steno pad back into my purse. I would go even though I hadn't finished studying and just fake my way through the study. That made me feel very guilty.

I picked up Charlie and Sammie from the sitter's, and Charlie babbled all the way home about getting a pine snake. He'd wanted a snake for a long time now, but I wasn't ready for a reptile in my house.

When I pulled into the driveway, I was surprised to see Max's car. That reminded me of my conversation with Shirl, which reminded me how good-looking Max was and how we'd had so little time together lately. Like he'd been avoiding me.

Charlie was still blabbering at me when I got out of the vehicle.

"It's just a little pine snake," he said.

"Not right now," I said as I walked inside the house.

"But —"

"No," I said again. "We've talked about this enough, Charlie. I told you, no snake right now."

"Maybe I should just go somewhere like a private school to live. Then I could have a snake. I could have anything I wanted." Charlie stalked past me, through the kitchen, and into the family room.

The phone started ringing before I could follow him and discuss his sour attitude. I didn't need this on top of my raging hormones.

Max walked into the kitchen. I blew him a kiss and yanked the receiver from the wall. "Hello."

"Patricia."

Only one person in the world calls me Patricia. Lady Angelica Louise Carmichael Cunningham, otherwise known as Max's mother. She's not a literal lady. She just plays one in real life. That's not nice to say, of course, but she's not nice. At least not to me. Max was passing behind me with his briefcase.

"Hello, Angelica."

Max put the briefcase on a kitchen chair and held out his hand. "Give me the phone," he mouthed.

"Hang on. Max wants to talk to you." I handed the phone to him.

Without even so much as a smile, he removed it from my hand.

"Mother?" he said into the mouthpiece. "I'm on my way to Dad's office now . . . no." After a pause, he glanced at me. "No."

Max was being more abrupt than usual with his mother. Normally they treated each other with cool dignity and just a touch of affection at special times, like birthdays and Christmas. On occasion he'd get irritated with her and treat her with gentle disdain, much like his father did. The only time I'd ever seen him angry with her beyond reason was when she had insulted me in front of him. She learned quickly. Now she waits until he's not around. She knows I'm not a sissy, and I'm not going to go whining to my husband. I like to settle my own differences.

I busied myself doing nothing at the kitchen sink so I could listen, but Max left the room with the phone. I was tempted to follow him. His odd behavior the last few days in combination with this cryptic phone call was enough to make me start a mystery notebook dedicated just to him.

As I emptied the dishwasher, Karen

passed through the kitchen on her way to work. "Hey, Mom, you're still working on the mystery, right?"

"Yes," I said.

"Good, because things are getting really bad at school. Mr. Slade wasn't there today."

"What?" I turned around. "He wasn't there all day?"

"No." She opened the door to the garage. "Oh, I'm going to the football game Saturday night."

"Sure, that's fine."

She left, closing the door gently behind her, and I turned back to the sink. Why had he led me to believe he had been at school today?

Karen's mention of the football game gave me an idea. Maybe I could collect clues there.

When Max returned to the kitchen, I stood in his path. "I'm going to the football game on Saturday. You want to go?"

Max raised one eyebrow. "You don't like football." He knew exactly why I wanted to go to the game.

I stuck my chin in the air. "I think I should support the school right now, given everything that's going on."

"Right," he said. "Yes, I'll go. If for no other reason than to watch out for you."

"That would be great." I paused. "Max, are you still attracted to me?"

He blinked. "Why would you ask me that?"

"Because Shirl said that you said I was eating three times as much as normal."

He laughed. "You are." He slipped his arm around me and pulled me into a hug. I opened my mouth to protest, but he leaned down and cut me off with a kiss. When Max sets out to deflect my attention, he does a great job.

It wasn't until after he'd left to take the kids to my parents' house that I realized he'd also deflected my attention from asking more about his mother's phone call.

During Bible study at church, one of the women brought up the scripture from Romans about food and eating, "If your brother is distressed because of what you eat, you are no longer acting in love." The group discussed this at some length, and I tried to fake my way through, but I was distracted by all the other things on my mind and couldn't concentrate. I didn't understand what that had to do with a lesson on the fruit of the Spirit, particularly love. Afterward, as I was leaving, Marion, the leader, called to me. My stomach clenched, thinking she noticed somehow that I hadn't done my work. I hated to disappoint her, she was so nice.

"Trish, I'm glad I caught you."

I smiled.

"I just want you to know how sorry I am that you're involved in such a tragedy. I spoke with Georgia on numerous occasions about the Lord when I went to visit her and Nettie, and I'm confident that no matter how horribly she died, she is now rejoicing in heaven."

My heart felt instantly lighter. I hadn't realized how badly not knowing that had bothered me.

"I'm on the school board, you know." She leaned closer to me. "I'm telling you this just to keep you from worrying about your children. Coach Smith and Marvin Slade have been put on administrative leave."

"Really?"

"Yes." She patted my arm. "Just know that I'm praying for you."

As I left the church, I felt warmed by her compassion, but that was mixed with anger. Why had Marvin led me to believe he was going into Connie's storage unit for school play purposes if he was on administrative leave?

12

One of the worst parts of pregnancy are the frequent doctor visits toward the end. Since I was starting my ninth month, I was now going each Friday morning to be poked and prodded in personal places.

The paper gown felt rough on my skin as I pulled myself up on the examining table. I determinedly avoided looking at my ankles. I was glad I couldn't see my rear end.

I wanted to distract myself from my fat flaws by rechecking my steno pad, but it was across the room in my purse, and I didn't feel like clambering off the table to get it.

I heard a knock. "Come in."

Dr. Williams breezed in and smiled at me. Her gray-haired bob was cut just below her ears. "So, Trish, how are you feeling?" She motioned for me to get into position.

"Oh, pretty rotten, really," I said. "I'm exhausted. My ankles look fat. My pants are tight. And I'm really cranky."

"That good, hmm?" When she was done with her exam, she patted my knee and told me to sit up. "Things look great with the baby. Right on target, although you need to remember that you had Sammie a couple of weeks early." She slipped her gloves off and dropped them into the wastebasket. "Everything you've mentioned is perfectly normal for most women. However, you've gained more weight than I would have liked. Especially within the last few weeks. I know you were thin to begin with, but gaining this much weight isn't good."

I wanted to sink through the floor. "Are you saying I'm fat?"

"I want you to stop eating for two now." She made a note on my chart. "Just cut out the sweets. That should do it." She closed my folder. "Do you have any other questions for me?"

"Yes. Would herbal teas help me?"

From Dr. Williams's immediate frown and the way she put her hands on her hips, I might as well have said, "Do you mind if I sniff glue?"

"Do not use anything like that unless you check with me first," she ordered. "Herbs . . . and drugs can be dangerous to babies. In fact, they can be dangerous, period."

I was discouraged. Even my doctor thought I was fat. To distract myself, I decided to hit up some places for advertising on my way back to the office. I started at the Shopper's Super Saver. Then I stopped at Bo's Burger Barn, where I bought some onion rings to soothe my emotions. The doctor had said no *sweets*. She hadn't said no onion rings.

I ended my trip at the dry cleaners where I always take Max's suits. The owner's daughter, a cute teenager, was behind the counter and smiled at me as I walked in. "Hey, Mrs. C."

"Hi." I put my purse on the counter and explained why I had come.

"I think Dad's already helping," she said. "We dry-cleaned some of the costumes for the play. Mr. Slade came and picked them up."

"He did? When?"

She bit her lip and thought. "Well, it wasn't yesterday, because I wasn't here. It was probably Wednesday."

The day before he came out to Four Oaks Self-Storage. Was he helping Connie work on costumes even though he was on leave? I shifted my purse strap to my other shoulder.

The owner's daughter put her elbows on

the counter. "You know, Mr. Slade acted really weird."

"Like how?"

"Well, I found some papers in the pockets of the clothes and put them aside like I always do. Dad drilled that into me for years and years. When Mr. Slade came, I handed them to him. He got all upset and grabbed them from my hands."

"Really? What were the papers?"

She shrugged. "Dunno. They just looked like receipts to me, and maybe some bills."

"Were all the clothes costumes?"

She frowned at me. "Dunno." Her gaze flickered over my shoulder as a buzzer signaled someone entering the shop. There probably wasn't much more she could tell me, anyway.

"Thank you," I said. "And I'll make sure to mention in the program that your father is helping."

"Thanks." She turned to the new customer.

My cell phone rang as I got into my car.

"Hello."

"Mrs. C.!" Heavy breathing wooshed through the receiver. "You wouldn't believe what just happened!"

"Shirl? Stop yelling. I can't understand you."

"The police were all over the place!"

"What?"

"The place was crawling with cops. Looked like an FOP meeting or something."

"FOP . . . what is . . . never mind. Just tell me what's going on." I turned the key in the ignition, my heart pounding.

"They searched Connie's units. All of them." Shirl was breathing so hard, it sounded like she was standing in a wind-storm.

"I'm on my way." I started to put my SUV in reverse.

"Wait!" she said.

"Shirl —"

"Just hang on. You shouldn't drive when you talk on the phone. You know how deadly that can be. It's bad enough people are keeling over at the high school and —"

"I'm about to get irritated with you," I said. "I want to know what's going on *right now.*"

"Hang on." She paused.

"Shirl?"

"Just hang on, I said. Mr. C. wants to talk to you."

I wanted to scream into the empty air.

"Trish." His deep voice sounded calm. "Hang on while I go to my office."

If one more person told me to hang on, I

was going to hang up. The phone clicked; then he picked up again. "Honey, Shirl's in an uproar, but things are fine." He laughed. "She loves drama."

That was an understatement. My heartbeat slowed. "Why were the cops there?"

"They said it was routine."

"They always say that." My mind went in a million directions. Had Marvin put something in a unit? "So they did search Connie's units like Shirl said?"

"Yes. It's part of the investigation. They had a search warrant."

I tapped my fingers on the steering wheel. "Are they gone now?"

"Yes."

"Was Detective Scott there? Did they take anything away?"

"Yes, he was here. And, yes, I think they took some things away."

Oh, I wished I had been there. "Is Connie a suspect?"

"Honey, I don't know," he said. "What I want to know is what the doctor said today."

"Oh, I'm fine. The baby's fine." I didn't mention how fat I was getting.

"Good. Well, I'm headed out to Baltimore. Shirl is calming down."

"Would you please tell her that I'll be there in about an hour?"

"Sure."

We exchanged telephone smooches, and after we hung up, I pulled my steno pad from my purse and made some notes. After staring at what I'd written for two minutes, I knew exactly what I had to do next.

13

That I would willingly appear in Detective Eric Scott's office was a minor miracle. He must have thought so, too, because his face was screwed up in a quizzical frown.

"Have a seat." He pointed to the chair in front of his desk. "You know we were out at Four Oaks Self-Storage this morning, right? We talked to Max."

"Yes, and that's why I'm here."

He took a deep breath. "We had a warrant." Dark, puffy circles under his eyes and the tension lines creasing his forehead made me inclined to feel sorry for him.

"I don't care about that. It's fine. I'm just here to help you."

He winced. "To help me?"

By his tone of voice, I could tell my offer of help wasn't welcome. My sympathy faded, and I bit back an angry retort. "Don't panic. It's just something you should know." I reached into my purse and pulled out my steno pad.

"Is that what I think it is?" he asked.

"My clue notebook." I licked a finger and flipped the pages.

A stream of breath hissed through his lips.

I glanced up at him. "Oh, come on. Stop with all the sighs. Can't you just accept the fact that I collect clues and quit making a big deal out of it?"

He shook his head. "No. You're a civilian. You're not a trained police officer. It isn't safe."

"You sometimes use informants, don't you? Besides, I came here of my own free will, out of the goodness of my heart, to tell you something. The least you could do is be friendly."

He tapped his pen on the desk and stared at me. "Fine. What is it?"

I put my finger on the page. "Connie just got her new unit last Tuesday. The day after the murder."

He pursed his lips. "Okay."

"On Thursday, Marvin came to Self-Storage with a key to look inside one of Connie's units."

"Shirl told us that," Detective Scott said. "And Max assured us that's on this side of legal. If someone has the key and the code."

"Yep. The thing is, he insinuated he was

there for school play business." I stared at the detective. "But he was already on administrative leave. He had no business there. If I had known that, I probably wouldn't have allowed him in."

"So?"

"Well, I did wonder if he was planting something or hiding something."

"Mmm," Detective Scott's eyes narrowed. "Anything else?"

I flipped to the page in my notebook that I'd just filled out. "I was at the dry cleaners just a few minutes ago. Connie had a bunch of costumes there to be cleaned. Marvin went to get them on Wednesday. That was the day before he looked in Connie's unit."

The detective stopped moving. "And?"

"The girl who works there said she had pulled some papers out of the pockets of a few of the costumes. She handed them to him. He got upset. Then he took all the costumes and left."

Detective Scott leaned forward. "What kind of papers?"

"She said some bills and some receipts and things like that."

He tapped his pen harder. "Trish, you shouldn't be —"

"I didn't purposely try to dig up this information. I went to the dry cleaners to ask them to advertise in the play program." I flipped through my notes. "Were you aware that people are saying Coach Smith helped football players cheat so they could stay on the team? And there are rumors that he used steroids." I bit my lip for a second. "In fact, some bagger kid at the Shopper's Super Saver insinuated that the coach was giving the players something."

Detective Scott cleared his throat. I met his gaze, but his eyes were shuttered. "What kid told you this?"

I shrugged. "I don't know his name. Spiky hair, piercings, tattoos, smoker, says 'dude' all the time, and looks and acts like he's done his own share of drugs."

"I see."

"That's all." I stuffed my steno pad back in my purse. "I'm trying not to get into trouble."

"Right." His sarcastic tone left little doubt of his opinion on that matter. He got up, walked around his desk, and stood by the door to his office. "Trish, I do appreciate the fact that you came to talk to me. That's good."

"But? I can hear a *but* in there."

He sighed again. "But I'm worried. This isn't a game."

"I'm not playing a game."

"Maybe you don't think you are, just like my daughter doesn't think she is."

I hiked my purse strap higher on my shoulder. "May I give you a piece of advice about your daughter, Detective?"

"Can I stop you?"

I glared at him. "Yes, you can. Just say no."

He closed his eyes and pinched the top of his nose; then he looked at me again. "I'm sorry. That was rude."

"Yes, it was." I debated saying anything at all, since he'd irritated me once again, but then I remembered the bitter tone in Sherry's voice when she talked about her father. "One thing I have experience with is being a parent to a teenager. It's not like sleuthing. It's something I really understand."

"So go ahead." He leaned against the door frame. "I might be able to use some advice."

His admission surprised me, and for the first time since I'd met him, he looked vulnerable. "Sherry is angry right now. What she could use is some unconditional love from you. Do some fun things together, Detective. Spend time with her, but don't spend that time nagging her or lecturing her." I took a deep breath. "Have you ever listened to her laugh? She's got a wonderful laugh."

He swallowed and blinked hard.

I smiled. "In order for a parent to really make an impact, a kid has to know how much they care. Communication with understanding is the key, even when the kid doesn't act like they're listening." I walked out the door; then I stopped and glanced at him over my shoulder. "That goes for adults, too, by the way. You can't expect people to read your mind about all the things you don't say."

My mother's farm kitchen smelled of roasting meat, boiling potatoes, and green beans cooked in ham stock, making me feel homey.

"I hope you're feeling better now," my mother said to me as she handed me a baking sheet for rolls. "I found out some things to help you solve this mystery, but I don't want to be blamed for killing my grandchild by putting you into shock."

"If finding Georgia didn't put me into shock, I doubt what you have to say will." I placed refrigerator roll dough that Ma had made earlier on the baking sheet.

"You can never tell," Ma said. "Could be something simple added to everything else, like building blocks. One last block on top of the pile, and the whole thing falls to pieces all over the place."

"Well then, be gentle with your blocks." I rinsed off my hands and put the rolls in the oven.

"Don't be smart with me, missy," she said.

"Sorry. But you can tell me."

Ma put her hands on her hips. "Well, if you pass out, don't blame me."

Sounds of the television came from the family room where the men were assembled. Men didn't work in the kitchen at my mother's house.

Ma put tea bags in a pitcher and poured boiling hot sugar water over them. "Well, Gail was talking to her hairdresser, whose daughter, Twila, is the principal's new secretary at the school."

"Mmm-hmm." She must have been the poor person Carla had called and barked at the day I'd been in her office.

"Well," Ma continued, "seems Twila comes home mad most days. That Bickford woman is impossible to work for."

"I can imagine. She comes across like a dictator."

"Hitler. Everything has to be her way. No one can have any thoughts but her." Ma turned and stared at me. "Thing is, that Carla was all buddy-buddy with Georgia, but not at the end."

"Really?"

"Yep. They had a big fight the day before Georgia up and got herself killed."

"What about?"

Ma shook her head. "Who knows? But Twila says Georgia tore out of Carla's office like she'd stumbled onto a yellow jacket nest."

Right then, Abbie's shadow appeared at the back door. I had a sense of déjà vu. From the time we became friends in kindergarten, Abbie loved coming to my house. She was raised by her grandmother, a very rigid woman who demanded more perfectionism than any kid was capable of. The woman had held grudges like kittens, bringing them out daily for feeding and petting. My mother might have a sharp tongue and be a master of manipulation, but at least I was allowed to be a kid.

"Hi." Abbie stepped into the kitchen, and I gave her a big hug. She smiled, but it didn't reach her eyes.

"Glad you could make it," my mother said to her. "Put your pocketbook down and cut the pork roast, please. You always do it best. The platter is right there."

Abbie obeyed. I checked on the rolls.

"You working on another book?" Ma asked Abbie.

"Yes." She sliced through the meat with a firm hand.

"Some crime thing?"

"Mmm-hmm."

Ma pointed at the beans, and I took the hint, turning off the heat.

"Well, you need to be careful with all that kind of thing," Ma said. "Crime and cops and things."

Abbie glanced over her shoulder. "Why?"

"Well, for one thing, that sheriff person was asking about you."

Abbie's body went stiff. I glanced at my mother.

"Detective Scott?" I asked.

"No, no," Ma said. "Not that one. Shorter, rounder. Looks like Santa Claus."

"That's Corporal Fletcher," I said.

My mother nodded. "That's the one. He's a pervert."

I choked and laughed at the same time, and it turned into a coughing fit. When I finally recovered, I stared at my mother in disbelief. "Corporal Fletcher? Ma, there's no way. He's a really nice guy. Why would you think that?"

She pursed her lips. "He was asking after Abbie. Did I know her? Was she available?"

"He asked you that?" I couldn't believe he would be so blunt.

My mother snorted. "Well, not in so many words, but I can read between the lines." She clucked her tongue and turned an indignant glance on Abbie. "He's married. Gail said he's got four kids and two grand-kids. You, young lady, need to be aware he's got his eye on you. Hard to believe, isn't it? He should be upholding the law, and here he is, an old married man, looking at you with lust in his heart."

I started laughing.

"It isn't funny." Ma's nostrils flared in indignation.

"I think you misunderstood," I said. "He wasn't asking for himself. He was asking for Detective Scott."

Abbie glared at me over her shoulder then turned back to the roast, slapping slices of pork on the platter as if she were swatting flies.

"How do you know that?" my mother demanded.

"Trust me," I said. "I know."

Sammie bounced into the kitchen. "I'm starving. When are we going to eat?"

"Let's talk about this after dinner," I suggested.

Abbie didn't say a word while we carried food to the table and avoided my glances.

After we were all seated and the food had

been blessed and passed around, Ma inhaled dramatically.

"I heard someone is coming in with a housing development," she said. "I don't know what things are coming to." She jabbed at a piece of pork roast on her plate.

"Can't say I'm real keen about a change like that, either," Daddy said.

Max glanced at me. "Change is inevitable."

I laughed. "Well, maybe Daddy can sell the farm and make a million."

My mother's head jerked in my direction. "Trish, how could you say that? I can't imagine . . . why —"

"I'm sure Trish was joking." Daddy's narrowed eyes gleamed a warning at me.

"Well, I should hope so." Ma glowered at me. "This farm will be sold over my dead body."

"Come on, Ma. Don't take everything so seriously." I hadn't expected such a strong reaction.

She grabbed the bowl of mashed potatoes and slopped some onto her plate. "Well, it's just that so many people are selling out. What's going to become of us? And what about my grandchildren? What if one of them wants to be a farmer?" The tone of her voice rose a notch. "What if *all* the farmers sell out?" Her voice broke from emotion.

"No one is going to sell the farm," Daddy said and lifted an eyebrow at me, which meant he wanted me to apologize.

"I'm sorry, Ma," I said obediently.

"Well, I should hope so." She huffed to herself for a few minutes while we all ate in silence. Everyone except Abbie. She was eating very little. Worse than anything else, she wouldn't look at me.

We were almost done eating when Charlie piped up. "Tommy might go to jail. And then I would go to a private boarding school to make sure I don't end up as bad as him."

Where in the world would Charlie get that idea? My mother-in-law?

Karen snorted. "You in private boarding school? They wouldn't take you."

"Tommy has love notes from a girl," Sammie chimed in.

The tips of Tommy's ears turned red. "I have no privacy at all."

Charlie crossed his eyes. "Tommy and Sherry sittin' in a tree, k-i-s—"

"Charlie, stop it." Max's stern, green-eyed gaze was enough to make Charlie back off.

Ma *tsk-tsked.* "I think it's amazing how much influence you have over those children, Trish. Charlie acts just like you did, all rough and ready to fight." Her expression grew speculative. "Tommy, do you have a girlfriend?"

Tommy mumbled something and stuffed a spoonful of mashed potatoes into his mouth. Max tactfully changed the topic, and my mother dropped the topic for the moment, but I knew I'd hear more. After supper she began whipping through the dishes in her usual efficient manner. I cleaned the counters. Abbie was drying pots and still hadn't spoken to me.

"So, is Tommy in love?" Ma asked. "I was a little worried about him. He hasn't had any real interest in girls."

"Ma!"

"Well, it's not normal. Boys his age should be falling in love every week." She grabbed the meat platter and sponged the grease from it. "Well, who is she? Someone I know?"

I sighed. "She's Detective Scott's daughter."

Abbie pursed her lips and rubbed the lid of a pot so hard I thought she would break off the handle.

"Oh my," my mother said. "And Tommy is a murder suspect? That's got to be awkward."

"He's not a murder suspect," I said.

"That remains to be seen. How the family will live down a murder trial is beyond me." Ma waved us toward the kitchen table. "Now you girls sit down and tell me exactly what's going on with all these policemen. What does this Detective Scott want with Abbie?"

I didn't know how much to say in front of my mother for fear that Abbie's potential love life would be a topic of conversation for the whole world to hear at Doris's Doughnuts. But on the other hand, if I didn't tell my mother something, she would speculate with Gail and April May about it for weeks in public.

Abbie's face looked like she'd been pickled.

"Okay, Ma. You gotta keep this quiet." I might as well ask a cow not to chew its cud.

Ma was indignant. "I don't gossip."

I'm always amazed at how out of touch people are with themselves. But that wasn't important right now. What really bothered me was the glare coming from Abbie's eyes.

"I'm sorry," I whispered to her.

My mother crossed her arms. "Just spit it out."

"Corporal Fletcher is asking about Abbie because Detective Scott is interested in her. He wants me to help get the two of them together."

"This is so humiliating." Abbie put her head in her hands.

My mother frowned. "Now don't you overreact. Nothing good ever comes from that. This Detective Scott, he's the tall one with blond hair, right?"

I nodded.

He's been coming into the store for years," she said. "What is he? Not a just a deputy, right?"

"Nope," I said. "He's a sergeant."

"He's not married, is he?" Ma asked.

"No, he's not. He's divorced."

Her breath hissed through her teeth. "How long ago?"

"About twelve years," Abbie said.

"How do you know this?" Ma asked her.

"Because he's been helping me with my books."

"Then why in the world wouldn't —"

"They've known each other a lot longer than that," I said.

Abbie eyed me over her hands, and I knew I was in big trouble.

"I see." My mother watched Abbie with a speculative gaze. "Well, I do know he's a good law enforcement officer. After all, he listened to Trish's advice during that whole Jim Bob Jenkins murder fiasco."

"Ma, he didn't listen —"

She waved her hands in a dismissive motion. "You're too modest, Trish. You solved that murder. And now you're going to solve this one." She leaned toward me. "I heard tell that Connie Gilbert, the principal, the coach, and that band teacher fellow have all been at the sheriff's office."

Before I could say anything, Sammie ran into the kitchen and begged Ma to come play a game with her. My mother's face brightened. She dried her hands and even left a wet pot in the drainer. Then she followed Sammie out of the room.

Abbie put her dish towel down and wouldn't meet my gaze.

"Abs —"

"I have to go. I have a book to write." She snatched up her purse and headed for the back door.

I followed. "I'm sorry."

The door banged shut behind us.

She whirled around to face me, gravel crunching under her shoes. "Did you agree to help fix me up with Eric?"

"I said I'd think about it."

"I can't believe it. You know how I feel."

"You've made it pretty clear."

"Of all people, you should understand." She looked like she might cry.

"I think I might understand better than you think."

"You're not acting like it." Abbie opened her car door.

I took a deep breath. I was about to cross a line, risking my relationship with my best friend. "This is deeper than Detective Scott. Or your emotions."

She tossed her purse onto the passenger seat.

"Don't you see?" I said. "You're becoming your grandmother."

Abbie's body stiffened, and she looked over her shoulder at me. "Did I just hear you right?"

"Yes, you did." My voice grew stronger. "Don't you remember? You said you'd never be like her, yet here you are, living by yourself, withdrawing from people, and walking away from a potential relationship with a guy because you have a grudge."

"I . . . don't . . . have . . . a . . . grudge." She climbed into her car.

"Yes, I think you do. For some reason, you're mad at him over something in the past. Has he apologized to you?"

"I won't talk to him about it," she whispered.

That confirmed my suspicions. "Did he try?"

"Yes."

I dug the toe of my shoe into the gravel. "Abbie, I know you might never speak to me again, but you've got to let it go. At least forgive him. There's a reason that's in the Bible. It's emotionally healthy. If you don't date him because he's not your type, that's one thing. But not because of something in the distant past. Look what grudges did to your grandmother. Remember her funeral? Who was there?"

I waited for Abbie to say something, but she didn't. She just jammed the key into the ignition.

"Call me when you're ready to talk." I turned around and walked slowly to the house, hoping she would call my name, but she didn't. The car door slammed, the engine started, and she sped out of the driveway.

My eyes filled with tears. I might have just lost my best friend.

14

Saturday was cleaning day. Everyone pitched in for two hours to get the house in shape. Then Max took the kids out in the afternoon without me — something he started months ago after we realized that Karen was resentful of all the attention he paid to me.

As I swished my mop across the kitchen floor, I thought about my bad parting with Abbie the night before, and I hurt, like a lead-weighted fishhook was hanging from my heart. I kept wondering how I could have said things differently.

I'd tried to call her all morning, but she didn't pick up, and I left five different messages. I was so distressed, I hadn't even bothered to write the information my mother had given me about Georgia's murder in my steno pad.

I was debating about driving to Abbie's apartment and banging down her door when the beep of my cell interrupted my thoughts. I dropped my mop and raced to get it, hoping it was her, but it wasn't. It was Sherry.

My whole body slumped. I had assumed she wasn't investigating anymore, because I hadn't heard from her. So her calling me now either meant bad news — that is, her father was rampaging even after my great advice to him, or she had more new clues. That would mean that sooner or later her father would be rampaging again.

"Hi, Sherry," I said.

"Did you know that Connie Gilbert is a suspect in Ms. Winters's murder?" She wasted no time on nonessentials.

"Yes." I dropped onto a kitchen chair.

"Well, Aunt Elissa is going to handle the costumes for the play. Ms. Bickford asked her to, and we're going to pick up some things from Connie today. Aunt Elissa thought you might like to come."

A distraction. That would be a better alternative than being arrested for bashing in Abbie's front door. Besides, with Elissa along, I wouldn't be responsible for Sherry's being involved in the investigation. That meant I'd be free to gather all the clues I could. Not only that, but I wanted to get to know Elissa a little better.

■ ■ ■ ■

Elissa drove her Mazda as though she were in a car chase on a reality cop show. The daredevil in me appreciated her skill. The mommy in me was scared to death.

Sherry must have sensed my emotions. She leaned forward from the tiny backseat and said, "Don't worry. Aunt Elissa has had training driving cars. She used to be a cop, like Dad."

Elissa was a cop? I glanced over at her.

"It's true," she said.

I didn't have a chance to pursue my questions, like why she walked with a cane, because she roared up Nettie's driveway and skidded to a stop, tires spitting gravel.

Sherry headed for the front door of the house, followed by Elissa. I walked more slowly, looking around. Nettie's farm had changed since I'd been here last. Contrary to what my mother believed, I did remember that she used to attend garden club meetings here. Even at that young age, I'd been impressed by the color-coordinated flower beds that Nettie had created. But now everything had changed. Weeds grew profusely in gardens that had once been tended with great care.

Elissa rang the bell. I joined her and Sherry on the front porch.

When Connie answered, she barely glanced at us. "Come in." She held the door open.

The wide foyer led into a gloomy, wood-floored hallway that was lined with furniture. On the right side, a staircase disappeared into the darkened upstairs. The air was stuffy and smelled of mothballs, toast, and the floral perfume I'd smelled in Georgia's classroom. It must be Connie's scent.

"I'm sorry about your loss," Elissa said to Connie once we were all inside.

Tears welled in her eyes. "It's been horrible. Georgia and I didn't always get along, but she . . ." She took a deep breath. "Well, I know you didn't come to listen to me cry."

"It's okay." Elissa patted her shoulder.

"I'm a suspect, you know." More tears glistened in Connie's eyes. "The police think I killed her."

Connie's tears might have been real, but in the dismal atmosphere of the Victorian farmhouse, I couldn't tell.

She turned to Elissa. "Thank you for doing the costumes. I suppose I could just decide not to provide costumes for the play, but I won't do that to the kids. Trish, I've lost one of the keys to my storage units. I'd really like to keep the one I have left. Would you like me to pay for a new lock?"

"I have a master," I said. "We'll use that."

She turned to Sherry. "Would you please give me a hand getting some boxes from upstairs?"

"Sure." Sherry responded eagerly.

Connie motioned with her hand toward a room to her right. "Why don't you two wait in the parlor while we get the costumes."

I was hesitant to let Sherry go alone with Connie, but Elissa didn't seem worried. While Sherry trailed Connie up the creaking wood staircase, I followed Elissa into the parlor, passing a long, narrow, marble-topped table in the hall, on top of which lay a bag from the drugstore.

Heavy red drapes hung on the tall parlor windows. Dark wood furniture and uncomfortable-looking velvet covered sofas filled the room. In true Victorian fashion, ornate tables were covered with knick-knacks.

Elissa turned a sharp eye to me. "I know what she's doing."

"Huh?"

"My niece." Elissa began walking the perimeter of the room, eyeing everything. "She's trying to solve this mystery. She's

218

worried about her boyfriend — your son. Corporal Fletcher told me." Her lips curled into a small smile. "He thought I might handle that piece of information better than her father."

Yea for Corporal Fletcher. I liked him better and better. The heaviness of responsibility for Sherry dropped from my shoulders. "Oh, I'm so glad. So you talked her out of it, right?"

Elissa laughed. "You're joking, of course."

"Well, I was hoping."

"No, I wasn't able to talk her out of it. Sherry comes by her stubbornness honestly. She'd continue even if we told her not to."

"Don't you think her investigating is dangerous?"

A flicker of concern passed over Elissa's face. "Yes, it could be. That's why I'm getting as involved as I can, especially with the play. I have a feeling things are going to get worse before they get better, and this way I can assure her father I'm taking care of her." She glanced around the room then gave me a quick smile. "Now let's get busy. Just don't touch anything."

I glanced at the coffee table and noticed a newspaper from Charlottesville, Virginia. "Look at this."

Elissa joined me.

"This is where Connie used to live," I said.

She stared at the paper. "Obituary section. Interesting."

Most of the deceased were elderly people, but one notice caught my eye. A very nice-looking man, maybe in his thirties. Aaron Bryant.

"Remember that name," Elissa murmured, pointing to the news photo.

Two thick books about antiques were piled on the other end of the table. I walked over to look at them. Peeking out from underneath the pile was a piece of paper on which I spotted a familiar fleur-de-lis.

I pointed at it. "I've seen something like this before."

Elissa joined me. "Oh, I recognize that. It's a receipt from a chain of pawn shops in Baltimore."

"I saw one of these on Marvin's desk at school," I said.

Elissa met my gaze with a frown, but before we could look more carefully at the paper, we heard Sherry's voice, followed by footsteps on the stairs. She and Connie were on their way down. No more time to snoop.

Their hands were full of costumes in plastic cleaner bags.

"I'll start carrying these out to the car," Sherry said.

Elissa nodded at her.

"Some of these costumes will need alterations," Connie said. "When the time comes, I'll need to show you how I do that without ruining the costumes. I have all the kids' sizes on forms that I left on Marvin's desk. I'll get those for you."

"That sounds good," Elissa said. "But are you sure you're up to it?" She nodded at the obituary on the table. "Have you lost more than one relative? That would be very painful."

Connie reached over to pick up the paper, her eyes tearing up again. "Well, in a manner of speaking." She swallowed. "Aaron and I were talking about getting engaged. It was a tragedy. He died the day before Georgia."

An elderly woman walked into the room carrying the plastic shopping bag from the drug store. "Did you bring this?" she asked in my general direction.

"I did, Granny," Connie said.

With gnarled hands, Nettie sifted through the bag. "I need my medicine." She turned to Connie. "Did you bring my medicine?"

"Yes. It's in there."

The older woman began pulling out the contents and strewing them on the couch.

Connie caught Nettie's arm. "Granny,

we'll get to all this in a minute. Wait until our company leaves, okay?"

Nettie held up a box. "What's this? A watch? Did you get a new watch?"

"Yes," Connie said.

"Why?" Nettie asked. "You had one. A pretty one."

"Yes, but I broke it." She took the bag from Nettie's hand and replaced the items inside.

"Where is it?" Nettie asked.

"I gave it to Aaron to get it fixed —" Connie's voice broke, and she pressed her fingers against her eyes.

I felt so sorry for her I didn't want to believe she was a murderer. "There are a lot of broken watches going around," I said by way of distraction.

"What?" Connie glanced at me.

"Oh, Carla broke her watch, too. One of the links. A beautiful thing. Gold. Looked expensive."

Nettie clapped her hands. "Carla. That's Georgia's friend. She comes a lot. We always have nice dinners." She paused and looked around the room. "Where is Georgia?"

My heart ached for her.

"Granny, it's time for your lunch." Connie placed the watch back in the shopping bag then turned to us. "I'm sorry. I really can't talk anymore."

"We understand." Elissa's expression matched my feelings — sympathy mixed with suspicion.

Sherry still hadn't come back, so we picked up the rest of the costumes to carry them outside.

Connie walked us to the door and murmured a quick good-bye as we stepped onto the porch. As the front door closed, Sherry walked around the corner of the house. She hurried over to me and took the costumes from my arms.

"Where were you?" Elissa asked.

"Checking out the gardens and stuff. Since Daddy implied poison, I was looking to see if there was anything suspicious. I didn't touch anything, though."

"And?" I asked.

"Well, there's this huge garden shed back there with all sorts of things in it. Squealing hinges . . . I was afraid someone would hear me. The shelves are filled with bags and bottles and stuff. Rat poison, bug poison. You name it, it's there."

We all climbed into the car, and Elissa turned the key, shifted into gear, and careened down the driveway. "There's something with the boyfriend," she said. "According to the article, he died very suddenly.

Seems strange that two people in Connie's life died without warning. It would be interesting to find out more about Aaron Bryant."

"And what about the pawn shop?" I explained to Sherry about the receipts. "Marvin said something about pawning school instruments the other day. But that wouldn't bring in a lot of money. Do you think Connie is pawning Nettie's belongings? There are a lot of valuable things in that house. And there were books about antiques on the coffee table."

Sherry had her head between the two front seats. "Maybe that's why Connie killed Georgia. To take the stuff and sell it."

Elissa glanced at her niece. "We don't know that Connie killed Georgia."

I frowned. "Besides, if Connie wanted money, she could have sold the whole farm. Georgia wanted to. Then Connie would have had half of everything. But she didn't want to."

"I'm going to make a few calls on Monday morning," Elissa said. "We're missing something here."

The Four Oaks High School marching band was leaving the field after halftime. The show had fallen flat, as if the band members were moving in a fog. The football team was losing. Jason had fumbled several plays. Without Coach Smith and Marvin Slade, the kids weren't holding together well.

I left Max with Charlie and Sammie on the bleachers so I could stretch my stiff body, as well as take a bathroom break — something that was occurring with more frequency. I noticed Detective Scott in attendance. He was in close conversation with a woman whose casual appearance didn't cover the fact that she was a cop. I desperately wished I could be privy to what they were talking about.

I passed Carla Bickford in a huddle with several parents. She was still wearing a suit, although this one was more casual, with pants and a loose jacket. I imagined her closet full of rows of suits, sorted by color.

Ten minutes later, when I was washing my hands in the bathroom, two women I knew by sight, who were also parents of high school students, walked in together. One had red hair that could only come from a bottle. The other was a natural mousy brown. They were so busy talking they didn't even look at me.

"She is just too big for her britches," the redhead said.

"Oh yeah. She thinks she's better than the

rest of us, that's for sure. I heard her family in Virginia was dirt poor."

The conversation stopped when they noticed me standing there.

"Trish, how are you?" the one with brown hair said.

I rubbed my stomach. "Besides feeling like I'm going to pop, I'm fine."

She nodded. "How awful about Georgia."

Both women watched me closely, and I recognized the look. They were eager for information and thought I could provide some, but I didn't want to. "Yes, it was awful."

When I said nothing else, the redhead began to speak. "My husband is on the school board, but I'm still thinking of removing our daughter from the school. Even with a police officer here, I just don't feel like it's safe."

The other woman nodded in agreement. "School resource officer, they call her."

I wondered if that was the young woman Detective Scott had been talking to earlier. "So she's assigned to the school now?"

"Just came on," the brown-haired woman said. "Has her own office and everything."

"Of course, Carla is going to do everything in her power to put a positive spin on this," the other one said. "Make it look like it was all her idea, even though it wasn't. It was the school board's."

"She's becoming a dictator."

That wasn't a stretch for Carla.

"Well, you know why, don't you?" the redhead asked.

"Yes. She probably wants to keep moving on. Leave her past behind."

They began joking about what kinds of pasts someone would want to leave behind. I'd learn nothing else here. Besides, I was hungry. I left the bathroom and detoured to the concession stand. There I considered buying a hot dog, which I love to eat with lots of onions and mustard. As I debated whether the momentary pleasure would be worth the price of acid reflux later, I caught a glimpse of Carla Bickford out of the side of my eye. She was stalking Marvin Slade, who was walking with two uniformed band members. I was surprised to see him, since he'd been put on leave. When Carla finally reached him, she tapped his shoulder. He whirled around and frowned at her. I wasn't close enough to hear their words, but I surmised from the way the two band members hurried away that the conversation wasn't pleasant.

Marvin's voice grew loud, and Carla pointed toward the parking lot. When he finally walked away, she patted her hair and headed for the bleachers. My curiosity got the best of me, and I followed Marvin, moving as fast as I could.

"Marvin, wait," I yelled.

His startled gaze met mine, and he hurried toward his car. When he reached it, I thought he might ignore me and take off, but his shoulders slumped, and he leaned hard on the roof of the car.

"Hello, Mrs. Cunningham," he said when I reached him.

"Hi." The baby was kicking my ribs again, and I felt a slight twinge in my abdomen. I wondered if it was a protest at any fast movement on my part. I needed to slow down. I opened my mouth to tell Marvin that I didn't appreciate his deception, but he started talking first.

"I know what you want."

"No, I'm not sure you do," I said. "I'm angry because you lied to me at Four Oaks Self-Storage. You led me to believe you were still teaching."

He smiled sadly. "The second part of that statement is the truth. I did lead you to believe that, but I never came out and said it."

"Sin of omission."

He shrugged. "What can I say?"

"So why were you there?"

He reached for the car door handle. "Let's just say, I'm a fool in love trying to save someone from herself."

"What?"

"In love for the first time in my life."

"Connie?"

He looked over my shoulder, and I saw his eyes flicker. He flung the door open and scrambled inside. "I gotta go."

He turned on the ignition and threw the car into gear. I backed away just in time for him to squeal away.

"If I didn't know better, I'd think he was avoiding me," a voice said over my shoulder.

I turned around. Coach Smith was standing right behind me. Based on the muscles in his shoulders and arms, I had no problem believing he took steroids.

"Did you want to talk to him?" I asked.

"As a matter of fact, I did. He's been snooping around . . ." His voice trailed off, and he looked at me. "But I'll catch him later."

"I thought you were on administrative leave."

The anger that lit his eyes frightened me. "I am. But I came to watch my team play. At least the kids will know I'm here." The big man turned and walked away.

I looked past him and saw Detective Scott, who watched the coach until he disappeared into the crowd. I headed for the concession stand, and the detective jogged over to join me.

I kept walking. "What do you want? Now everyone here will think I'm guilty of something."

"No, they won't." He entered into step with me. "I'm human, too, you know. I do talk to people about things besides police business. I even have friends, although that might be hard for you to believe."

He had a point there. "So you're walking with me just to shoot the breeze?"

"No." He smiled down at me. "I do have a purpose, but people don't have to know that. I want to know what you and Marvin were talking about."

I stopped abruptly and looked up at him. "I told him I didn't appreciate him lying to me. Then he said something very interesting."

"And that was?"

I explained what Marvin had said. "You know, that's really weird. I think he's talking about Connie."

"Mmm." Detective Scott nodded. "Did the coach say anything?"

"He insinuated that Marvin was snooping

around."

"I see."

We began walking again. The young woman he'd been talking to earlier motioned for his attention. Before he left, he looked at me. "Trish, be careful."

I met his serious gaze. Then he turned away, and I returned to the concession stand.

"Tell me you're not thinking about a hot dog with onions," a voice said in my ear. "You know you'll suffer all night." Max looked down at me. "How about I buy you a hot dog with just mustard?"

Shortly, Max was carrying drinks for four, along with a bag that contained two funnel cakes. Charlie and Sammie helped me carry five hot dogs. The kids were chattering, but I wasn't paying attention to them. I'd stopped in my tracks, as had everyone else around me.

There, in the shadows next to the bleachers, Detective Scott was kneeling on the ground with his knee in Coach Smith's back, handcuffing him. The young woman the detective had been talking to earlier stood in a typical cop stance, with her gun pointed at the coach's head.

15

On Monday morning, I was so glued to the local news for information about Coach Smith that I didn't pay attention to Max until he kissed me good-bye.

I looked him up and down. He was wearing his best charcoal pinstripe suit. "A meeting?"

"The board of directors," he said. "Lunch and a meeting afterward. But first I have to stop at the office in Rockville."

"Okay. That's good to know. This afternoon I have to go by the high school and drop off all the advertisement agreements, so I'll be leaving work a couple hours early."

He nodded as he clipped his cell phone to the holder on his belt.

I turned back to the television in time to see the wholesome, blond newscaster purse his lips in an expression of disgust.

"Coach Kent Smith of the Four Oaks High School was arrested on Saturday night for suspicion of providing drugs to minors," he said. "He's still in jail pending arraignment today."

"I guess they didn't let him out on bail over the weekend," Max said as he opened the garage door. "They'll probably set bail today, and he'll be out."

"They should lock him up and throw away the key," I murmured.

As I drove to work, I thought about Coach Smith. I needed to update my clue list with all the information I'd gathered over the weekend. Townspeople's speculation was rampant, and I'd gotten an earful at church the day before. The coach had murdered Georgia because she found out what he was doing. He was part of a bigger drug ring with ties in Baltimore. And then there was my mother's favorite broken record. He was the head of an international crime ring that had infiltrated our town to bring in gambling casinos.

Based on what I knew, I tended to believe he'd been arrested for providing drugs to some of his players to improve their performance. I remembered the newscast I'd seen about a performance-enhancing drug and wondered if that was the one he'd given them. No matter what, arrest was too good for a man who would do that to teenagers.

Whether he murdered Georgia remained to be seen.

When I pulled into the parking lot at Four Oaks Self-Storage, I was so focused on my speculation about Coach Smith, it took a moment to register the fact that a shiny red Mercedes was hogging Max's parking space. I knew who it belonged to, and I wanted to make a fast U-turn. As I opened the front door of the building, I caught a whiff of Chanel. My mother-in-law's favorite scent.

Shirl was standing behind the front desk, hands on her hips and a scowl on her face. She motioned with her head toward the closed door of Max's office. "Her Highness is in there," she whispered.

"What does she want?" I whispered back. "Is she waiting for Max? He's not planning to be here today."

Shirl shook her head. "She was asking when you were going to come into work." Shirl paused and sniffed. "I had some messages for Mr. C., so when I called to give him those, I told him that *she* was making herself at home in his chair."

So Angelica was here to see me. Shirl knew and was trying to protect me. A nervous quiver sped up my back.

From the side of my eye, I saw the office door open, and Angelica's perfectly made-up eyes met mine. "Patricia? Will you please join me for a moment?" Her cool, cultured voice always annoyed me. Possibly because I couldn't achieve the same effect, no matter how hard I tried. She didn't wait for me to answer, just turned on her Gucci heels and disappeared again.

Her tone of voice, combined with the way she presumed to take over Max's office, obliterated my nervousness.

I handed my purse to Shirl, but before I could enter the lion's den, she patted my arm. "Don't you worry none, Mrs. C. You got more class on a bad day than she does on her best."

I didn't agree, but I met her gaze with gratitude, and she smiled. That gave me the extra push I needed. I strode into Max's office, shutting the door behind me. Whatever Angelica had come to tell me, Shirl didn't need to hear.

Angelica was seated behind Max's desk. Without an audience, her smile was gone. In its place was an icy frown. However, if she thought that would scare me, she was mistaken.

She sniffed gently. "I came by to pick up some papers for Max and his father about the new housing development, but I'm glad you're here. I have something I need to discuss with you."

It took every ounce of my fruit of the Spirit self-control not to gasp. "Housing development?"

"The one they have planned for Four Oaks." She raised one delicate eyebrow. "You mean, Max didn't tell you?"

I refused to make it appear as though Max had kept this a secret from me. "Oh yes. That."

"Please sit down." She pointed at a chair in front of Max's desk.

"If you don't mind, I'll stand."

"Do as you like. You usually do. But you might wish to be seated when I tell you this."

The gloves were off, so to speak. I knew for sure this conversation wasn't going to be pleasant.

"Your father-in-law and I want to see that Charles goes to a private boarding school in Bethesda."

"What?" I locked my knees.

"He is, after all, our youngest grandson."

I couldn't catch my breath, like the time I fell off a swing when I was little and had the air knocked out of me. Suddenly everything was clear. Max's hidden papers and behind-closed-doors phone calls. Charlie's attitude and comments.

Angelica's mouth was set in a slight smile.

"I felt you should know. Particularly since your actions precipitated our decision. Of course, I warned Max when he married you."

Not only were the gloves off, but she was flexing her claws. "My actions? What do you mean by that?"

She shook her head as though I was an unfortunate, stupid child. "You can't stay out of trouble. You allow the children to run wild. Their futures are at stake. It's too late for Thomas, but it's not for Charles. I talked to Max a few days ago and have started making arrangements at the school."

I remembered my mother's comment that I was influencing the kids and not always positively. That made me feel guilty, but unlike many people, when I feel guilty, I don't crumble. I get mad. The Bible study about the fruit of the Spirit flickered through my mind, but I dismissed its words of wisdom.

"Does Max know you're telling me this?" I could barely see her for the red haze in front of my eyes.

She sighed. "No, he doesn't. Whenever I talk to him about it, he adamantly defends you."

Well, at least he did that.

"But I'm going to insist," she added.

Her tiny smile made me truly regret I

couldn't lapse into the Trish of years ago. I allowed myself the luxury of imagining how good it would feel to fling myself across the desk, tackle Angelica, and throw her to the ground. I'd yank her hair, messing up her perfect hairdo, pulling until she screamed. The temptation was so great, I leaned forward, clenching and unclenching my fists.

Fortunately, before I could do anything, the door opened behind me. Angelica's smile died.

I stepped back, away from temptation. "I'm not going to discuss this further with you. Max can tell me the rest."

"The rest of what?"

I turned. Max was frozen in the doorway. When no one spoke, he walked over and stood next to me.

"Trish?" He squeezed my shoulder.

I met his gaze, but I couldn't see for my tears. I couldn't believe he'd betrayed me.

"Ask your mother." I jerked away from him and rushed from the office.

He didn't follow. I heard his voice rumbling and could tell from the tone that he was angry.

So was I. At him and his whole stupid, stuck-up family.

Shirl wasn't even pretending to work. "Mrs. C., is there anything I can do?"

"No, thank you. Just hand me my purse."
She did.

As I opened the front door, I said over my shoulder, "I'll be gone for a while."

I felt sick and vulnerable as I pulled my SUV from the parking lot. Where could I go to hide from everyone? I desperately wanted to go to Abbie's, but she still hadn't returned my calls. I could think of only one other place I would feel safe.

When I pulled up to my folks' farm, I thought Daddy wouldn't be there, but I was relieved to see his truck parked near the barn.

After nearly falling out of the SUV, I stumbled over the rough ground and pulled a side barn door open, unable to see clearly through the blur of tears in my eyes. Buddy the border collie greeted me first. My gaze followed the sound of Daddy's distinctive off-key humming to where he was pulling the contents out of some white metal storage cabinets. He'd been using them as long as I could remember, repainting them every five years.

"Daddy?"

He whirled around at the sound of my voice. "Sugar bug, what are you doing here? I thought you'd be at work."

"I was, but —" My lower lip started to tremble.

He wiped his hands on a cloth and crossed the expanse between us with large strides.

I couldn't do anything but stand there and cry.

He put his hands on my shoulders and looked me up and down. "What's wrong, honey?"

I swallowed and sniffled. "I . . . I can't really talk yet."

Worry darkened his eyes. "But the baby's okay? Nothing's happened to anybody?"

I hiccupped. "Everyone is safe." Buddy licked my hand, and I scratched his head.

"Okay." He dropped his arms. "You just take a minute and get yourself together, then tell me what's going on." He waved toward the junk on the floor. "I could use the break."

I inhaled. "Lady Angelica . . ." I felt a tear on my cheek. "Well, she came by the office and told me she wants to put Charlie in boarding school. Because I'm a bad mother."

Daddy snorted. "Who does she think she is? The queen?"

"Probably," I murmured. "Daddy, I was really tempted to grab her and beat her up. It took everything I had not to do it. Maybe

I really am a bad mother. What kind of grown woman thinks things like that? And a Christian woman to boot."

A quick grin passed over his face. "You'd be surprised." Then he frowned. "So, what does Max have to say about all of this?"

Fresh tears burned my eyes. "That's the thing. I'm not sure." I inhaled. "He showed up shortly after she told me, and I left him there. I was just so angry that he hasn't said anything to me about this. Why wouldn't he tell me?"

"That's a good question."

"And that's not all. You know that housing development Mom has been yakking about?"

Daddy nodded.

"Well, Max and his dad are behind that." I rubbed my arms. "Why didn't he tell me about this, either? Why did I have to hear it from Her Royal Highness?"

Daddy shook his head silently.

"And now Tommy is being investigated for murder. And Abbie won't speak to me anymore because I said she was acting like her grandmother." I was close to wailing.

The muscles in Daddy's jaw worked, a sure sign he was holding back what he really wanted to say.

"Is there something wrong with me?" I

met his gaze. "Why wouldn't Max trust me?"

Daddy took a deep breath. "I can't say what Max was thinking. Sometimes, though, men are fools."

I couldn't keep my tears under control. "I . . . I need to be alone for a little while. You mind if I sit up in the loft?"

He brushed a piece of hair from my eyes. "You don't even have to ask. You go. And I'll be praying. For all of us." Daddy rarely got mad, but I saw a spark of anger in his eyes. His defending me made me feel good.

"Thank you," I whispered.

"Can you get up there okay?" He looked down at my belly.

"Yeah. I'll go around to the top."

He didn't try to stop me, and he held Buddy so he wouldn't follow me. One thing about my Daddy, he knew me well enough to know what I needed. He'd always been sensitive that way, helping to counteract my mother's sharp tongue.

The loft was warm and smelled of hay and livestock. I realized I should have gotten a drink. My mouth felt sticky. I'd get some water in a little while. For now, I pulled myself up onto a hay bale and leaned against another. I closed my eyes and let the smell of the barn roll over me. Hay, cattle — all of it comforted me. This was where my roots were. I was a farm girl, a redneck. And proud of it. But despite growing up and all the changes God had made in me, I was afraid that underneath it all, I'd always be a girl who was ready to fight at the drop of a hat. I wanted so badly to act kind, to be a godly Proverbs 31 woman. But how could I when I was overwhelmed by my feelings?

Had I made a mistake when I married Max? Was I denying his children their true birthright just by being their mother? Or worse, had he been so desperate for his kids to have a mom that he settled for the first available woman who came along at church? Max and I had some problems in the past, but nothing like this. Our love and passion had been enough to overcome our differences, and I'd assumed we'd always have that. But now I wasn't sure. I wondered if his recent secretiveness, combined with his lack of attention, was an indication that his decision to marry me had been nothing more than rebellion against his upbringing. I'd always had that fear in the back of my head. That he'd get over his initial attraction to me and be sorry we got married. Was that happening now?

Tears spilled down my face, spotting the

shirt that stretched over my swollen tummy. I felt another twinge, and the baby kicked. I closed my eyes, praying in desperation.

Several minutes later, when I heard the distinctive purr of Max's car pulling up to the barn, I wasn't surprised. He knew me well enough to eventually figure out where I'd go. I sat up straight and waited.

16

The rumbles of Max's voice and Daddy's angry replies came up through the floorboards of the hayloft. During each lull in their argument, I expected to hear Max's steps on the ladder, but then the two would start all over. Gradually, though, I heard only murmurs.

When Max finally climbed up to the loft and appeared through the square entrance in the floor, I turned my head away from him.

He walked across the wood floorboards and stopped in front of me, looking down. "I'm sorry."

A blanket apology. Was that supposed to make everything okay? I refused to meet his eyes, just stared at his feet, thinking how strange his shiny black shoes looked on the rough, dusty floor. I studied his laces in an effort to distract myself enough to avoid crying or losing my temper. I was in danger of both.

Max shifted from foot to foot, but I didn't invite him to sit down. "Your father reamed me out."

"Yeah, I heard."

I wasn't sure what to say next, and he must not have been either. The silence stretched into several minutes as I pulled pieces of hay from the bale under me, bent them in half, then crushed them and tossed them to the floor.

I couldn't stand the silence any longer. "You should have told me everything. You don't trust me."

"That's not true."

"Then why couldn't you tell me any of this?" I asked through clenched teeth.

Max sat on a bale of hay next to mine, but he didn't touch me. "I didn't tell you about the housing development because we were still trying to figure out if it was feasible."

"And you couldn't talk to me about it?"

"I knew how you'd feel, and . . ." He paused and took a breath.

"And what?" I asked.

"I knew how you'd react." He glanced at me and shrugged. "I didn't want to fight about it until I knew there was a reason to fight. I'm sorry. I just wasn't up to that."

"You didn't want to fight. . . . Am I that hard to get along with?"

"Honestly? Sometimes. Especially lately." He shifted on the bale. "We're both a little touchy right now."

"What about *Charles* and the boarding school? Were you afraid to tell me that, too?"

Max nodded. "As far as I was concerned, that was a nonissue. The idea was Mother's, and there was no way I was ever going to agree to it."

"You should have told me anyway."

He inhaled. "Yes, probably. But . . ."

"But you were worried about my reaction to that, too?"

"In a word, yes."

I could add this to my recent list of failures. Not only was my husband holding back the truth from me because he was afraid I'd overreact, but my best friend wasn't talking to me because I'd hurt her feelings with my big mouth. My mother thought I was a bad influence on the children. My mother-in-law agreed with that, too, which led, of course, to her implication that Tommy was a criminal. Not only that, but I wasn't working on a Bible study I so obviously needed. I felt like the biggest loser in the whole world — and that made me even madder.

"And . . . there's something else," Max said.

I looked up at him, so angry I felt sick. "What else could there possibly be?"

He took a deep breath. "Well, Dad wants to partially retire. He wants to turn more of the business over to me." Max glanced at his watch. "In fact, that's what this board meeting is about. I have to leave pretty soon."

That figured. Even now, in a crisis, business would come first. I knew I was being unfair, but I couldn't help my thoughts, which only served to prove that Max's comment about my irritability was right. "Well, can you spare sixty seconds to tell me why your dad wants to semiretire?"

Max ignored the sarcasm in my tone. "He had a scare not too long ago. He thought he had cancer." Max paused and swallowed. "When the doctors said the tumor was benign, Dad decided it was time to start enjoying life."

"The tumor?" I felt like the bottom of my world had fallen out, but anger surfaced again. "And you couldn't tell me *that,* either? Something that bothered you so badly?"

Max spread his hands. "Dad didn't want

me to tell anyone. Not even Mother. She just found out, which is probably why she had that outburst in my office."

For once in my life, as impossible as it seemed, I felt sorry for my mother-in-law. "So that's where you get your secrecy from? Your father? What is this? Some sort of secret, manly Cunningham society, even though we agreed — no more secrets?"

Max blinked, and his eyes glinted bright green. "I don't think it's secrecy. I just don't see the reason to address issues until it's necessary."

"As far as I'm concerned, they become issues as soon as you become aware of them."

"Sorry, I don't agree." His lips snapped shut. He was as angry as I was.

"I'm your wife, Max."

His cell phone rang. He sighed, pulled it from his belt, and looked at the screen. "That's Dad." He gave me a quick glance. "I need to get it."

"You do that." I stood to my feet.

He reached for my hand. "Trish."

I backed away before he could touch me. The phone kept ringing.

He pushed the button. "Hey, Dad. Hang on. . . . No, I'm not on my way yet. . . . Yes, I know I'm supposed to be there shortly." Max put his hand over the mouthpiece.

"You go on and talk," I said.

Max looked like he was deliberating then held the phone to his ear again.

"It's fine, Max." My voice cracked. "I have some things to do at work. Besides, I can't talk about this anymore."

I whirled around and headed for the big open doors at the front of the barn. I heard the thud of Max's heels behind me, along with his voice on the phone. I knew I shouldn't walk away, but I was hurt and — once again — acting out my anger. I needed to get away from him before I said anything I'd regret.

"I'll tell you what," Shirl said as I stepped into the office. "You should have been here for that showdown between Mr. C. and Lady Angelica."

"I'm glad I missed it." I pulled some bills from the mail on the counter.

"You've been crying, haven't you?" She looked me up and down. "I'd like to give that woman a piece of my mind, what with you being pregnant and all. What was she thinking? Are you sure you should be here?"

"Yes. I'm better off working, believe me. Besides, after lunch I need to drop some forms off at the school for Carla."

Shirl turned and glared at her computer

monitor. "I'm not so sure *I'm* better off being here. I've got one fine kettle of fish to deal with." Her fingers *tap-tap-tapped* on the desk.

I didn't want to know what was wrong. I couldn't care less right now, as upset as I was with Max, but I debated whether I should ask Shirl what she meant. If I did, it could end up in a very long conversation in which I didn't want to be involved. Like about her herb business. Still, if I didn't ask, she'd corner me at some point anyway. Besides, she'd stuck up for me this morning.

"So what's wrong?"

"Connie's check is bouncing all over the place."

Of all the things Shirl might have said, I wasn't expecting that. "I'm surprised."

"Ha. You shouldn't be. It's a habit, I'm afraid." Shirl slapped her palm on the counter and glared up at me over her glasses. "She said it would never happen again, and I believed her. She's been good for a while now."

"You mean she's bounced other checks?"

"Yes. And I'm not going to cut her any slack anymore. From now on, it's all credit card payments or she's out of here. I don't care if she does rent all those units." Shirl's chin trembled with indignation.

Shirl's loyalty to me, Max, and our business was the reason I loved having her work for us. She might be annoying, spinning off in so many directions I could hardly keep track, but she was like a guard dog when it came to our finances. When I took time off after the baby was born, I knew Shirl would run things just fine.

"I know you'll do the right thing." I took some bills from the counter and began to walk to my office when Shirl's voice stopped me.

"And to make things worse, that Coach Kent Smith got out on bail."

My stomach flip-flopped. Did that mean we had a murderer loose in Four Oaks?

When I heaved my body through the front door of the high school, I headed directly for the office, carrying my folder of forms.

There I saw Sue, one of the school secretaries, eating a candy bar. I didn't recognize the other secretary.

She looked up at me with a frown. "Yes?"

"I'm here to deliver these to Carla. Can I leave them with you?"

"No, that's not a good idea." Her nameplate said TWILA. Carla's unhappy secretary.

"How come?" I asked.

"It would be better if you delivered them to her in person. If you leave them with me, she's going to be mad because I saw them first. Or something stupid like that."

Things *were* bad. "Okay, where is she then?"

"She's gone to see if rumors are true that Coach Smith was here talking to some kids. She also chasing down Connie Gilbert, who got here a little while ago, and she also mumbled something about seeing Marvin in the band room. Carla has *nothing* good to say about Connie. They recently had a telephone yelling match. And *Connie* was here to chase down Marvin Slade to get the play's costume list from him." She paused for a deep breath. "He gave his notice today and was cleaning out his desk. Lucky him."

Sue nodded and swallowed a bit of candy bar as she nervously glanced toward the hallway through the glass wall. "She's upset because her fiancé died."

"Connie's fiancé?" I asked.

"No," Sue said. "Carla's."

"What?" Way too many people were dying.

Twila jabbed a pen into the blotter on her desk. "To tell the truth, I was surprised she even had a fiancé. I mean, who would want her?"

"Don't say that." Sue took a nervous gulp from a can of soda.

"Whatever." Twila sniffed. "This school is like some sort of Peyton Place. Georgia admiring the coach's muscles in the gym, dating him a couple of times, then having nothing else to do with him. Marvin sniffing after that costume woman, although that's better than last year when he dated most of the females working here. And Queen Carla mourning over Ronnie. I wonder if he even existed. No one ever met him."

"You better be careful what you say." Sue glanced around as though checking for secret cameras.

Twila exhaled with exasperation. "I don't care anymore. It's always all about her. Her life. Her fiancé. Her, her, her. She's so possessive. I don't even dare touch any of her stuff. My first day on the job, I took her coffee cup from her office and washed it out, and you'd have thought I'd committed the unpardonable. Really, Sue. You and I should just walk out."

"I can't afford to do that," Sue whined. "I got kids and haven't gotten an alimony check in months."

Twila rolled her eyes.

"Well, she *is* going on vacation, remember?" Sue said. "Like tomorrow or the next day. Sort of spur of the moment."

"So, what do you guys think happened to Georgia?"

They turned and looked at me as if they'd forgotten I was there.

Sue's eyes grew round. "I think she was poisoned. By Coach Smith. For dissing him."

Twila shook her head firmly. "I don't think so. This is one thing I agree with Carla about. Georgia's death was an accident. No matter what the cops say. She was always drinking these herbals teas she mixed up at home. A special blend that gave her energy and suppressed her appetite. You gotta be careful with things like that. Too many stimulants can kill you."

"I still think it was Coach Smith." Sue surprised me by defending her opinion. "The guy was freaking out when Georgia refused to date him anymore. Or it was Marvin. He asked me out once." She shivered. "You know, I could be dead right now."

"Well, with the coach, it was just his ego," Twila said. "He had other girls, believe me. A lot of good they'll do him in jail."

As the two debated, I decided to go chase down Carla and get this over with. I left the office just in time. The secretaries' conversation had moved into a discussion about how Coach Smith was probably going to come back, shoot them all dead with a shotgun, spalttering the walls with blood.

My mouth still felt dry, and I needed a drink of water badly. I was about to go in search of a vending machine when I saw Tommy heading my way.

"Hey, Mom." He had half a doughnut in his hand.

"Hi, honey." I stood on my tiptoes and pecked him on the cheek, figuring it was fine since no one else was around. "Where'd you get that, and what are you still doing here?"

"Trying to keep my part in the play." He grinned sheepishly. "We just finished practicing with the new teachers in charge. I'm sucking up to everyone. I brought doughnuts." He took another bite.

"Did you see Marvin Slade?"

Tommy's smile died. "Yeah. Just a couple minutes ago. It's really sad. He was in the band room packing his stuff. I left him some doughnuts, too."

"Where's Sherry?"

He shrugged. "Probably in the auditorium. I left right after practice."

"Well, aren't you two — ?"

256

"Mom, the way things are right now, I can't go there, okay?"

I blinked at the vehemence in his voice. "Has Detective Scott questioned you again?"

"No. And I'm going to do my best to make sure he doesn't have to." Tommy edged away from me. "Listen, I gotta go now. Gotta get to work." He turned and jogged on up the hall, and I resumed my walk toward the band room.

When I passed the doors to the auditorium, I saw teenagers were milling around the room. Sherry was there, too, and she looked up and waved at me. I waved back, even as I picked up my step and hurried on, trying to avoid her, but it did no good. She made a beeline for me, rushing out into the hallway.

"Hi, Mrs. C. I have a message from Aunt Elissa for you."

I slowed down, and she fell into step next to me. "What's that?"

"Well, seems that receipt you guys saw at Connie's was from a pawn shop in Baltimore. They have a number of things there that fit the description of things that are missing from Nettie Winters's house."

I stopped in my tracks. "You're kidding."

She shook her head. "Aunt Elissa thinks

either Connie or Georgia was pawning things. I wonder if it wasn't Connie and she murdered Georgia because she found out. And that's not all."

"What else?"

"Well, that boyfriend of Connie's? The fiancé? He died in a suspicious death. It looks like someone broke into his house to rob him and shot him to death."

I began walking again, trying to piece things together in my mind.

"I think Aunt Elissa is helping Dad or something, because before she talked about the whole thing with me, but now she won't. And she's been in to talk to Ms. Bickford. Everyone's a traitor, I guess." She paused. "Mrs. C., have you seen Tommy?"

I glanced at Sherry. "Yes, he's on his way to work."

"He's ignoring me." Her mouth quivered like she was going to cry.

I touched her arm. "You understand why, don't you?"

Her eyes flashed, and her lips firmed. I knew exactly how she was feeling and felt very, very sorry for Detective Scott. He'd better handle the situation differently, or he would drive her away.

"I'm going to clear Tommy's name once and for all." She crossed her arms. "I don't care what anybody says. Then, when we practice our kiss, I won't feel like I'm pressing my lips on a cardboard cutout. When we first started practicing, there was some real feeling."

Oh, great. That's all I needed to hear about. Passionate kisses between my son and a girl. I wanted to clap my hands over my ears and say, "La la la la la la, I can't hear you," but that would have been too obvious. Instead, I glanced up at the ceiling so I could recover my equilibrium.

"Mrs. C.?"

"Mmm?" I twisted my head, trying to decide if the brown water stain right above my head looked more like a dog or a cow.

"Are you mad at me, too?"

The tone of her voice was so forlorn, I felt terrible. I met her gaze again. "No, I'm not." I knew what it was like to be in love with a Cunningham man. Once it happens, you just can't help yourself.

"Where are you going?" Sherry asked.

"I'm looking for Carla — Ms. Bickford. Her secretary said she was meeting Marvin in the band room. She was also looking for Connie."

"I'll come with you."

I began to argue with her but decided I wanted company. With the school practically empty, I didn't want to be alone with my imagination.

"We have a substitute band teacher," Sherry said as we walked toward the band room. "And someone else is taking Ms. Winters's class for the rest of the year."

"Your aunt will still be doing the costumes, right?"

"Yeah. Aunt Elissa wants to talk to you about that. She wants your help."

When I reached the band room door, I had a weird sense of déjà vu. I didn't like the chill that crept over my head, making my hair feel like it was standing on end. Sherry's presence offered small comfort, especially since I was responsible for her safety.

I pushed the door open. The lights were on. So was a DVD, playing the movie *Arsenic and Old Lace.*

"Carla?" I called.

No answer.

"Marvin?"

No answer.

"This is sort of creepy," Sherry said.

"Yeah, tell me about it."

A box of doughnuts lay on Marvin's old desk. Beside that was a packing box partially filled with music books. Then I noticed splotches of liquid dotting the floor next to

260

a shattered ceramic mug and a half-eaten doughnut.

Sherry's breath hissed through her teeth.

From the television, Mortimer Brewster said, "You . . . Get out of here! D'ya wanna be poisoned? D'ya wanna be murdered? D'ya wanna be killed?"

The words were ironic given that Marvin Slade was in a heap on the floor.

17

Slouched on a chair in the hallway of the school with my eyes closed, I felt heavy, like someone had opened the top of my head and poured in concrete. With emergency personnel and cops in and out, I paid no attention to the sounds of the footsteps around me until someone stopped next to me.

I opened my eyes and looked into the eyes of Detective Scott.

"I might have known." His tone was resigned.

I wasn't surprised to see him. Sherry had called him as soon as we discovered Marvin on the floor. I tried to sit up straight, but I didn't have the energy. "He's okay, right? He had a pulse. I watched the paramedics take him away."

"He's alive." Detective Scott's gaze searched my face. "How about you? How are you feeling?"

"Numb."

"You're pale."

"Probably just shock."

His searching gaze made me feel defensive.

"I had a good reason to be here, you know."

"I'm not surprised. You usually do."

The heaviness in my legs increased. "Tommy did, too."

He drew a sharp breath. "Tommy was here?"

Me and my big mouth. Still, Detective Scott would find out sooner or later. "Yes. He was bribing teachers with doughnuts."

I didn't like the look on the detective's face. Corporal Fletcher appeared, and when I tried to smile at him, my mouth wouldn't work. I took a deep breath, and my vision turned to spots. I began to slide out of the chair.

"Oh, hey!" The corporal rushed forward and grabbed me under the arms.

Next thing I knew, I was laid out on the floor, and Detective Scott was kneeling next to me with his finger on my pulse. "Fletcher, get the paramedics."

"Yessir." The corporal walked down the hall, talking into the mike on his shoulder.

My mind felt muddled. "No ambulance,"

I whispered.

"Yes, an ambulance," Detective Scott said.

"I don't want to go to the emergency room." I spoke louder and tried to clear my vision. "You don't understand, Detective Scott. They know me by name there." I felt the baby kick. I forced myself to relax and take deep breaths.

Detective Scott stared at me, eyebrows in a deep V. "Would you please just do something without arguing? Just this once?"

Since I had just slid out of the chair, I decided to agree. "Okay."

"Okay?" His eyes widened. "Just like that? Okay?"

"Yes. Okay." I took another deep breath and felt the fog in my head lifting. Maybe I just needed to remember to breathe. "How is Sherry?"

"Fine." The way he answered told me he was annoyed with her.

I met his gaze straight on, or tried to. "Don't blame her, Detective. Neither of us was investigating. I was here to find Carla to deliver advertising commitments. Sherry was just walking with me. She's a good girl, you know, but she's very vulnerable right now."

He closed his eyes for a moment then opened them again. "I know."

I decided to let the topic drop. There was only so much I could do for either of them, and now wasn't the time for an in-depth conversation. I took more deep breaths and began feeling a bit better.

"I'm going to need to question you, but it can wait until later on," he said.

"It wasn't just an accident then?" I asked. "Was Marvin attacked? Like hit? I didn't see any blood or anything."

Detective Scott stared at me, and I could almost see the cogs in his brain working. "I don't think so."

I felt a brief sense of relief. "I was afraid Coach Smith had come in and bashed Marvin over the head." Then I realized what the detective had said. "What do you mean, 'I don't think so'? Do you think someone did something to Marvin? Like, he ate something funny?" I began to panic, thinking about Tommy and the doughnuts. "He probably had a heart attack. I know that ―"

"You need to calm down." Detective Scott patted my arm.

"I hate it when people say that to me." I struggled to sit up.

In a gentle manner that belied his irritated scowl, Detective Scott reached an arm around my shoulders, helped me sit up, then propped me against the wall.

Corporal Fletcher joined us again, and the detective stood.

I looked up at both of them. "Do you think this has anything to do with Georgia?"

"Stop talking," Detective Scott ordered.

"Yes, but what happened to Marvin? If he wasn't bashed in the head, then was he poisoned? Coach was out on bail." I looked up and down the hall, expecting to see Carla marching around giving orders. "Where is Carla?"

"On her way back," he said. "She'd gone home."

"What about Connie? She was here, too, you know."

Detective Scott exchanged glances with Corporal Fletcher, whose forehead was creased with worry. "We're not going to discuss this right now. I'll come by your house later." The detective motioned to another deputy. "Watch her until the paramedics get here." He crooked a finger at the corporal. "Fletcher, come with me. I'm afraid this is my fault, although I told Marvin not to come here."

Linda Faye King, the emergency room nurse wrapped the blood pressure cuff around my arm. "Well, we haven't seen you in quite some time. I figured you were trying to be careful, given you're pregnant and all, but here you are."

The implication, of course, was that I was still as foolish as ever, even risking my baby's well-being.

"I'm just a little dizzy is all," I said. "I think maybe I hold my breath when I get stressed. And . . . I've had a few tiny pings in my abdomen. Probably Braxton Hicks."

"Lots of people have false labor pains, but we'll see." She pursed her lips and pumped up the cuff. "Dizziness can be a sign of lots of things. Like the placenta could be detaching, and the baby could die."

Fear gripped my stomach. "Well, I'm not —"

"Well, your blood pressure is fine. That's a good sign." She paused. "You know, we had a lady in here last week who lost her baby. Poor thing. Stillbirth. Imagine."

I was going to throw up.

"The lady's mother was already in here with some sort of heart palpitations. Those coincidences happen a lot — like Nettie Winters and her niece a couple weeks ago." Linda Faye efficiently folded up her blood pressure cuff. "I mean, can you believe that? All in one family? On the same day?"

"I'm not sure I follow." And I couldn't

imagine she should be telling me all this stuff, but then again, she always did have a big mouth.

"Connie was in here, too — the same day as Nettie. Heart pounding."

I had another wave of dizziness.

"And here we are again," Linda Faye continued. "You and Marvin Slade here at the same time. Then the police were here, too, and —"

The curtain to the room was swept aside by Bill Starling, our general practitioner and regular physician at the hospital. Linda Faye shut up like someone had slapped her. That's what I thought. She shouldn't have been telling me all of this.

"Surprise, surprise." Bill smirked. "Imagine seeing Trish Cunningham in the emergency room. I guess I'd better call your obstetrician."

Max appeared behind Bill. That's when I started to cry.

Two hours later, I sat on my bed, wearing one of Max's old shirts over black leggings. Whenever I feel insecure, wearing something of his helps me, even now, when we were still at odds. My favorite pink, cross-eyed bunny slippers lay on the floor, and I was wrapped up in my favorite afghan.

268

The baby was fine. For that I was very grateful. But my doctor said I had to be careful now, especially because I'd been having minor contractions. I was also dehydrated and probably stressed. They'd given me fluids to get my metabolism back in order.

I'd had some problems with dizziness at the beginning of my pregnancy, as well, so my present reaction wasn't totally unexpected.

"Honey? You awake?" Max walked into the bedroom carrying a cup of hot chocolate and my steno pad, my Bible study, and a pen. "I thought you'd like these." He set everything down on the nightstand and stood next to the bed.

"Thank you." I reached for the hot chocolate and took a sip to avoid meeting his eyes.

We hadn't yet spoken about our argument earlier in the day. We were awkward with each other, a little like acquaintances instead of husband and wife. I suspected that his bringing my notebook was a form of apology. Besides which, he probably thought I'd be writing down notes anyway, so he might as well accept it.

"We need to talk, I guess." I put the mug back on the nightstand.

"Yes." He brushed a strand of hair from

my face. "But not now. Let's do it later when we won't be interrupted."

"All right." Normally, I like to get things over with, but I was glad for the reprieve. I still felt too raw and hadn't had time to sort things out in my head.

His eyes watered. "Baby, just know that I love you more than anything in the world. If anything happened to you . . . Well, we'll work all this out."

Tears came to my eyes. I leaned against him, and he hugged me.

Karen appeared at the bedroom door. "Mom, are you okay?"

"Yes, honey." I saw the worry in her eyes and felt bad. "Really, I'm just fine."

She smiled. "Good. Grandmom is here. She brought Charlie and Sammie home." After a last glance at me, she turned and left.

"I have to go see to the kids." Max headed for the door talking over his shoulder. "Your mother is making dinner."

"Do the little kids know what happened?"

"I'm not sure if your mother told them or not. If not, I will." Max stopped and turned around. "I want you to know that I'm going to try to stop the housing development project. I don't know if I can, but I'll try."

"Max —"

"I didn't bring it up to discuss it right now. But you're more important to me than any business venture. That's the least I can do."

As I watched him leave, I wasn't sure how I felt about the whole thing anymore. I still felt betrayed by his lack of trust in me, but how much of that was my fault?

A few minutes later, buoyed by the warmth of the hot chocolate and the green and white afghan, I finally relaxed. The baby was pressed up against my ribs, making it hard to breathe, but I didn't care. I was just grateful everything was okay.

I picked up my Bible study book and opened it to the latest lesson. The main scripture was 1 John 3:18: "Dear children, let us not love with words or tongue but with actions and in truth." The words niggled at my brain. I knew there was something the Lord was trying to tell me, but the words grew blurry under my tired gaze. I set the book aside, rolled over on my side, and drifted to sleep, only to be awakened shortly by the sounds of my my mother's voice and my youngest children's footsteps on the stairs.

"Land sakes. Your mother is a magnet for crime lately. But then she's always been in trouble. Did I ever tell you kids about the time she was twelve, and she took Abbie for a ride in her granddaddy's truck? Gonna herd cattle, was what she said later. I thought my heart would stop in my chest when I saw the two of them rolling by in the pasture, cattle scattering to the wind and . . ."

I'd heard that story approximately ten thousand times. So had everyone else in the family. While she stood just inside the doorway, droning on and on, Sammie and Charlie burst into the room. Sammie caught herself just before she jumped on the bed. I hugged her and eyed Charlie over her head. His lips were in a thin line, and his body was tense.

"I'm fine," I mouthed at him.

His body relaxed.

When my mother was finally done with her narrative, she put her hands on her hips. "Well, missy, you managed not to kill my latest grandchild."

"Everything is fine." I hoped she wouldn't keep hounding me. I wasn't up to sparring right now.

She stared at me, eyelids blinking. In a flash of perception, I realized she had been worried sick about me and the baby. Because her tongue is so sharp, I tend to forget she's vulnerable.

"I'm sorry to worry you," I said.

She shrugged. "Well, I should be used to it. Now, you're going to rest tonight. I'll take care of everything here. I'll call you when it's ready." She motioned to Charlie and Sammie. "Come on, kids. Let's cook."

"Thank you," I whispered. She didn't hear me, but I wasn't thanking just her. I was also thanking the Lord. I had a lot to be grateful for, and lately I seemed to have forgotten that.

I'd been ordered to be still and rest, but that didn't mean I couldn't think. I grabbed my clue notebook and pen from the night-stand.

I had a lot of clues to write down.

Carla bullies Twila. Carla was buddy-buddy with Georgia but had a fight with her the day before Georgia was killed. Carla has a fiancé named Ronnie who gave her a watch. My four main suspects have all been at the sheriff's office for questioning. Is Marvin in love with Connie? Coach was arrested for giving drugs to kids. Georgia dated Coach a couple of times then dumped him. Receipt at Connie's was from a pawn shop in Baltimore. Connie had a boyfriend named Aaron Bryant who was killed in Charlottesville the day before Georgia was murdered.

As I tapped my pen on my bottom lip, my

mind went back to Marvin. Maybe he had a heart attack. Shirl said he was talking to the pharmacist about heart medications.

Nothing made sense to me.

While I was staring at what I'd written, I saw motion at my bedroom door and looked up.

Abbie was standing in the doorway.

18

Abbie didn't move. I remembered when we were little, spending nights huddled together with a flashlight under the covers during weekend sleepovers. Whispering all the secrets that little girls keep. As we got older, giggling about boys and the other girls. In many ways, she knew me better than Max ever would.

"Do you mind if I come in?" she asked.

"You have to ask?" I could hardly breathe.

She approached my bed slowly. "I wasn't so sure you'd want to see me."

"Why would you think that?" I put my notebook on the bed beside me.

"I figured you were mad at me. I haven't returned your calls."

I shook my head. "I was afraid I'd driven you away." I sniffled back tears. "I've got such a big mouth. I'm sorry."

"No," she said. "I'm sorry."

She held out her index finger, and I held

out mine. We touched the tips. Our old sign of friendship. When we were little, we'd pricked our fingers, made them bleed, and held them together. Blood sisters.

Abbie is rarely demonstrative, so that meant more than any words she could say. Relief poured over me. I hadn't ruined one of the most important relationships of my life. "How come you didn't answer the phone?" I mumbled into her shoulder.

"Because I went away. I had to have time to think." She let go of me and straightened up.

I sat back and wiped my nose with my bathrobe sleeve and pointed at the green upholstered chair next to the dresser. "If you can stay, grab that and pull it over here."

She did, shook her shoes off, and propped her legs on the bed.

"Where'd you go?" I leaned back against the headboard.

"To the beach. I sat on the balcony and watched the waves." She sighed. "I concluded that you're right. I'm turning into my grandmother."

I wiped my nose again on my sleeve. "Does that mean you'll date Detective Scott?"

She laughed as she snatched a box of tissues from the bed stand, took one for herself, then handed the rest to me. "I don't know about that, but I am going to deal with some of the issues in my life." She wiped her nose. "Now what's up with you and Max?"

I laughed and blew my nose, then leaned back against the headboard. "How did you know something's up?"

"Because of the way he told me to come up and see you."

I explained our fight to her. When I was done, I took a deep breath. "Am I really that big of a grump?"

She glanced at me then glanced away. "You've always been kind of prickly, but right now you are worse than you've ever been."

I felt so small. "I'm going to have to apologize to him. I hope he'll be able to forgive me."

"Well, you can't take all the blame. He does have that arrogance thing going on, and he should have told you these things despite your grumpiness." She smiled. "But he adores you. You guys will get it straightened out."

"I hope so."

"Trust me."

I rearranged the pillow behind my back. "Now will you tell me why you won't date

Detective Scott?"

Abbie's lips narrowed, and I raised my eyebrows at her.

"All right, all right. I'll tell you. Then I want to let it go for a while, okay?"

"Fine."

"It's not that I don't like him. Not at all. In fact, the opposite is true."

"Well then —"

"Eric was the one who told me that my husband was cheating on me. They worked together, you know."

I nodded.

"My husband cheated one too many times. I couldn't take it anymore, but Eric tried to talk me into staying with the marriage. When I walked out, Eric was mad. It was like a good ol' boys' club." She paused. "I thought he was my friend. I thought he'd support me."

"So you felt like he was judging you?"

"Yes. And then he ended up going through a divorce himself."

"Did he apologize?"

"Yes, he did." She swallowed. "I refused to forgive him. . . . At least I refused then."

"And now?"

She took a deep breath and met my gaze with a quick smile. "Now I'm ready to do the right thing. Whatever it is that God wants me to do. Walking in God's love instead of selfishness sometimes means doing the very thing we don't want to do. In my case, that's leaving the past behind."

Abbie's words struck me like a physical blow.

"Did I say something wrong?" she asked. "Your face is all screwed up."

I shook my head. "No. You said exactly the right thing. That's what the Lord has been trying to get through to me." I snatched my Bible off the bed stand and opened it to 1 John 3:18. "Listen to this, Abs. 'Dear children, let us not love with words or tongue but with actions and in truth.' "

She smiled. "That's it, exactly."

She put Bible back on the nightstand and picked up the notebook "Now I want to hear about your mystery. Maybe I can help."

I laughed. Abbie had helped me solve Jim Bob Jensen's murder by providing me with an essential piece of information she had gained from researching her crime novels.

She flipped my notebook open. Her eyes widened, and she glanced up at me. "Wow. I'm impressed. This is much more detailed than your last list."

I felt absurdly pleased by her remark. "That means a lot coming from Ms.

I-Outline-My-Books-in-Gory-Detail."

She grinned. "Does Max know you're investigating?"

"Yes. He said he can't stop me."

"I believe that." She leaned back and studied my notebook. Then she handed me the notebook and steepled her fingers. "To sum it up, Marvin might have just had a heart attack and it wasn't a murder attempt at all. He's possibly involved in a drug scheme. He's also in love with Connie. Connie stands to inherit Nettie's farm now that Georgia is dead. Oh, and her boyfriend is dead, too, so maybe she murdered two people. Either Georgia or Connie was pawning Nettie's belongings, and Marvin might have been in on it. Maybe he and Connie murdered Georgia with poison.

"Then there's Coach Smith. Besides giving kids drugs, he was dating Georgia, and she dumped him. Carla is a selfish control freak who wants to be better than she is." Abbie flicked the pages with her fingernail. "I wonder how many of them knew about the drug and/or cheating scheme?"

"That's a good question." I sighed.

"Love and greed are powerful motives," Abbie said.

An hour later, we were seated at my dining room table finishing up a meal of fried chicken, mashed potatoes, gravy, and corn pudding. That wasn't going to help my waistline, but I enjoyed it. Since I came downstairs, Sammie had been glued to my side and insisted on sitting next to me at dinner. Charlie had been eyeing me while he continued his usual chattering. Tommy and Karen were at work.

Ma was beginning to clear the table with Abbie's help when someone knocked at the front door. Charlie scampered to get it.

I heard a familiar man's voice and Charlie's higher pitched one jabbering excitedly.

"Hey, look. It's that policeman," he announced as they walked into the dining room.

At that moment, Abbie entered the room through the kitchen door holding an apple pie. Her eyes connected with Detective Scott's. I was afraid she would drop the plate.

He broke eye contact first, shifting his gaze to Max and then to me. "I'm sorry to interrupt. I'd like to talk to you, but I can wait outside until you're done eating."

I had visions of him huddled in a dark, cold car while we sat inside eating apple pie and drinking coffee.

"I'm done." I stood slowly to my feet. "Let's talk now. How about we go into the living room?"

Ma burst out of the kitchen with coffee mugs, which prompted Abbie to plunk the pie on the table. She whirled around and went back into the kitchen.

"What is he doing here?" Ma asked nobody in particular. "Trish has to rest. No more cops and robbers for her today."

Detective Scott smiled. "I won't keep her long."

Ma's fisted hands rested on her hips. "Well, I should hope not. I'm sure she's already helped you plenty. You need to solve the crime so she can have some peace before this baby comes."

I looked over at Max whose expression was resigned; then I looked at the detective. "Let's go get this over with."

Max accompanied us with his hand on the small of my back.

When we got to the family room, Detective Scott eyed me with drawn cheeks and a wrinkled forehead. "Are you okay to do this?"

"Yes. I'm feeling great now. Have a seat." I pointed to one of the overstuffed chairs.

"Thank you." He settled into the chair's depth, reached into his shirt pocket, and pulled out his small notebook and a pen.

I sat on the sofa, and Max sat next to me.

"I was very concerned about you earlier today," Detective Scott said. "I'm glad you're okay."

"Me, too," Max breathed.

I put my hand on his leg, and he put his arm on the sofa behind me.

Detective Scott shifted in the chair. "I want to know what happened from the time you walked into the school."

I told him. Then I mentioned running into Tommy in the hallway.

As I spoke, Max's body stiffened. He looked down at me. "Tommy was there?"

"Don't worry," Detective Scott said quickly. "Tommy is no longer a person of interest. Neither are any of the other students. In fact, after the first day or two, they weren't suspects. We just needed information from them." He paused and eyed me. "That's between you and me."

The detective was finally trusting me with something. I also felt like a load of bricks was lifted off me. Max did, too — I could feel his body relax.

Max removed his arm from around me. "In that case, perhaps I should go get the kids ready for bed. Will you be okay, Trish?"

I nodded.

When he was gone, I focused on the detective. He was studying his notes; then he looked up. "Did you speak with anyone else?"

Sherry. I felt panicked, wondering how he was going to react when he found out that his daughter was still trying to solve the mystery. My foot starting wiggling in response to my nerves.

"What is it?" he asked.

"Well, Sherry and I talked."

We were interrupted by Abbie who walked into the room carrying a tray on which were two mugs and two plates holding thick wedges of pie.

"We thought you guys might need something." She set the tray on the coffee table then straightened and met his gaze. "You look tired."

"I am."

"I know this has got to be difficult." She took a deep breath. "When you get done with this case, why don't you give me a call?" She quickly leaned down and kissed my cheek. "I'm going home now. I'm glad you're okay."

As she walked from the room, Detective Scott followed her with his eyes. They shone with a mixture of hope and anxiousness like a teenage boy's. However, once she was out of sight, the expression disappeared, and he turned to face me.

"So, what about Sherry?"

"She was looking for Tommy. He's avoiding her because of you. It upsets her."

The detective's jaw tightened. "What did she say?"

I told him, leaving out the part about Sherry wanting to kiss Tommy. That fell under the topic of *too much information* and meant nothing to the investigation. He didn't seem surprised by what Sherry told me, which made me wonder if she was correct. Elissa was helping her brother.

He tapped his pen on his leg. "I'm going to walk through the whole thing with you again. From the time you pulled into the parking lot."

I nodded and felt a sudden admiration for him. His personal feelings and obvious weariness weren't deterring him from his job. I could learn a lot from his self-discipline. I took a deep breath and answered his questions as he prompted me. He was particularly interested in the conversations I'd had.

When I was done, a tiny grin played on his lips. "Now, is there anything in that notebook of yours that you'd like to share with me?"

I couldn't believe he wanted to know what I thought. I retrieved it from my bedroom.

He flipped through the pages and even jotted something down. I tried not to let my sense of satisfaction show, but when he smiled at me, I think he knew how I felt.

A few minutes later, after he left, I went in search of Max. He was talking to Tommy, who had just returned home, so I went upstairs and got ready for bed. After I got under the covers, Max walked into the bedroom. "After my shower, we need to have that talk."

19

I leaned back against the headboard, picking my nails and listening to the water run in the bathroom. I knew what I had to do. Apologize. But first, I needed to get one other thing cleared up. By the time Max walked back into the room, I had worked myself into a minor dither.

He sat on the bed and grabbed my hands. "Stop picking. You'll make yourself bleed."

I sat up straight. "Max, I'll never live up to your family. I'm a redneck through and through. I'm afraid you're going to wake up one day and wish you hadn't married me. Your mother always insinuated I forced you into it. Did I? I didn't do anything but fall in love with you. In fact, I tried *not* to fall in love with you. But if I hadn't done that, then I wouldn't have Sammie. Or Karen, Tommy, and Charlie. And this one." I rubbed my big tummy and felt my lower lip tremble. "That would be awful."

"Where is all this coming from?" Max let go of my hands and put his fingers under my chin, forcing me to look at him. "I've never regretted being married to you. You're my balance. You keep me from becoming what my family is." He paused. "Well, at least my mother."

"Don't you think I'm a bad influence on the kids?"

He smiled. "You're the best mother our kids could have."

I blinked back tears. "Really?"

He laughed. "Yes. Your spontaneity and daring is what I love the most about you. You've helped them not be afraid of things. Especially Tommy. Remember how he was when I first married you? The nights you insisted on sitting up with him?"

I thought about the skinny little boy Tommy had been then, tormented by nightmares. "Yes. I love him," I said softly. "I love all our kids."

"I know that." Max stroked my hair. "I didn't even consider my mother's suggestion to put Charlie in a private boarding school. The idea was absurd. The kids need you — they need us as a family. That's why I didn't say anything to you. Besides, you didn't need another reason to dislike my mother."

"But Charlie knew, didn't he? He threatened once that maybe he should go to private school."

Max grimaced. "Unfortunately, my mother said something to him. But I straightened it out. He doesn't really want to go."

He kissed me, walked to his side of the bed, and got under the covers.

I rested my head on his shoulder.

We lay in silence for a few minutes. I inhaled the scent of soap on his skin and felt the slow thump of his heart.

"I'm sorry I've been acting like I have been. So grumpy you couldn't even tell me about the housing development. I've been very selfish."

He sighed. "Well, you were right about that. I should have told you." He stroked my hair. "I'm sorry."

"Have you talked to the board about stopping the project?"

"Not yet. I haven't had time." He shifted. "You know, come to think of it, I think that housing development is one of the reasons that Georgia had it in for Tommy."

"What?" I lifted my head and looked at him. "What do you mean?"

"She wanted to sell the property badly. Nettie was in no condition to make decisions. Dad and I heard about it and approached her. She must have gotten her hopes up. When we determined that the property didn't meet our criteria, she was furious." He sighed. "Connie didn't want to sell. That's why I talked to her that day at Self-Storage. To make sure she understood we weren't going to buy it. She was happy."

"Maybe that's because she was pawning stuff. Someone in the house was." I put my head back on his shoulder. "But if it was her, then why?"

"That's a good question."

Lying with Max in the dark, hearing his soft breathing and feeling his protective embrace, reminded me again how much I loved him.

I took a deep breath and steeled myself. "Max, don't stop the housing project. I know you were doing that just for me. You don't have to. I'm fine."

He inhaled sharply.

"I mean it. Like you said, it's going to happen. It might as well be you and your dad first."

He turned onto his side. "Are you sure?"

"Yes."

"Thank you." He kissed me and pulled me tight. "I've missed spending time with you like this. Time alone."

"What?" I struggled to a sitting position. "You haven't tried to spend any time alone with me lately. Cuddling used to be such a big part of our lives. Now you barely look at me."

He frowned.

"I know it's because I'm fat," I moaned. "And my ankles are fat, too. My pants are tight. I just can't help it. And I eat like a horse. I —"

"Baby . . ."

"Well, I do. And I feel so ugly and —"

He grabbed my hand. "Trish, hush."

"It's true," I whispered.

He pulled me close again. "I'm so sorry. I wasn't reading your signals right."

"What do you mean?" I tried to pry myself loose, but I couldn't.

"Well, you kept telling me how badly your body hurt and how tired you were. I just assumed you didn't want anything to do with me — that you just wanted to be left alone."

"But you were acting like you were avoiding me."

"No." He groaned. "Not at all. I didn't want to bother you. You have no idea how hard the last month has been."

"Really?"

"Really."

I finally untangled myself from his arms.

"So you don't think I'm the fattest, ugliest thing you've ever seen in your whole life?"

He laughed. "No. Not at all. I'm nuts about you. I always have been. And I think you're beautiful."

I didn't go into work on Tuesday or Wednesday in an effort to rest as ordered. That meant no excuses for not completing sewing for the baby's room. But, by midday Wednesday, I thought I would go insane. The only thing saving me was knowing I was going to help Elissa and Sherry begin to sort through play costumes that afternoon.

Yellow fabric slid under the needle of my whirring sewing machine as I finished a seam on the last set of curtains. My mind was whirring as fast as the machine. I'd tried to call Marvin at the hospital, but he didn't answer his phone. I couldn't find out from anybody what had really happened to him. I kept running all my clues over and over in my head.

I was done with the curtains and had started the ruffle for the bottom of the crib when my home phone rang. I grabbed the portable off the wall in the kitchen.

"Well, I'm glad you're home and not risking my grandchild's life by going to work today."

"Hi, Ma. I can be taught."

She snorted. "I have my doubts about that. What are you doing?"

"Sewing. Then I have to help Sherry and Elissa Scott with costumes for the play."

"You're going to drive?" she demanded. "You know we're having high winds. Where are you going?"

"To the high school. It's not a long drive. It can't possibly hurt anything."

"That place is a bastion of murder and mayhem," she said. "You should pull the kids out."

"Everything is locked down now. During the day only the front door is open, and the resource officer sits there at a desk. After school you can't get in unless you have an appointment. It's safe."

"Well, locks don't stop bad people. In fact, seems to me it would just encourage them to break in. And what if the bad guys are in the school already? We're surrounded by all sorts of criminals, you know." Ma paused. "That's why April is on leave for a few days."

"We're surrounded by criminals, so April's on leave?"

"Yes."

"So, what's the crime?" I asked.

"Just like I said. Gambling. See? People should listen to me."

As usual, my mother's conversational technique made me feel as if I had brain whiplash. "April is gambling?"

"Oh, for heaven's sake. Not April. You should know I'd have better sense than to hire someone who gambled."

I bit my tongue so I wouldn't ask the obvious question: How can you tell when people are gambling — do they have it written on their heads? "Well, who then?"

"It's Connie. *She's* been gambling. Online."

"Connie's gambling online. . . . What does that have to do with April being on leave?"

"She's got to take care of Nettie, of course."

"Where is Connie? And why can't she still watch Nettie?"

"Connie's been stealing stuff from Nettie to pay off her gambling debts." Ma huffed indignantly. "Can you imagine? The family had her arrested last night. Today they're having a big family meeting to figure things out."

Pieces of the mystery puzzle began falling together in my head, but I wasn't sure they were making a complete whole. This did possibly explain April's comment that

Nettie was misplacing things. Perhaps it hadn't been Nettie at all. Instead, Connie was taking things to pawn. And was Connie gambling online in the school library? If Georgia had discovered what Connie was doing, that would explain Georgia's anger and their fight in the library. Was Connie the murderer? And that brought up Marvin. He had a copy of a pawn shop receipt on his desk. Was he in on this with her?

"Have you heard anything about Marvin Slade?" I asked.

Ma snorted. "Oh, that one. Yes. This morning Gail's cousin's wife came by. Her husband is on the school board. She told Gail that Marvin was out of the hospital today, but they think maybe he was involved in the drug scheme. You know what they're saying, don't you?"

"No. That's why I asked." I tapped my fingers impatiently on the kitchen table.

"Don't get smart or I won't tell you," she said.

I doubted that. She could never stand not sharing a juicy tidbit of gossip, but I apologized anyway.

She sniffed. "The drugs Coach Smith used were for performance all right, but not just sports. They were supposed to help the kids take tests better. Something called Inderal. People take it for their hearts. Can you imagine? What will they think of next? Coach Smith claims Marvin knew all about it and was helping kids pass tests by cheating."

Now I was really confused. Cheating. Gambling. And a drug called Inderal.

"That principal woman was here this morning to get coffee. Oops. I have to go. We have customers." Ma hung up before I could even say good-bye.

I needed more information. I picked up the phone and called my doctor's office.

20

A half hour later, my cell phone rang. Sherry's name popped up on the screen, and I hit the TALK button.

"Hey, Sherry."

"Mrs. C., are you still coming to help with costumes this afternoon? Ms. Bickford told me this morning before she left for vacation that she didn't think you'd be coming because you'd been in the hospital."

"I'm still coming. Is your dad okay with you doing that at the high school?"

"Yeah," she said. "Aunt Elissa will be there, and that seems to make him feel better."

That made me feel better, too. Then a thought occurred to me. "I hope we don't have to work in the band room."

"Oh, no," Sherry said. "That would be awful. We'll be in the auditorium behind the stage. And I'll meet you at the side door nearest the auditorium to let you in. Umm, but I have a favor to ask you."

"What's that?"

"Can you go by Ms. Gilbert's house and pick up a few more costumes? We're missing a couple of things. Somebody named April said she found what she thinks we need. Aunt Elissa is at some sort of meeting and will be coming straight here, and my car still isn't working right."

I agreed. I'd be perfectly safe going to Nettie's house, since Connie wasn't there. I promised to be at the school in an hour and a half.

At Nettie's a flustered but smiling April opened the door before I could even knock. That was good. The wind was blowing something fierce, sweeping leaves across the overgrown lawn and whipping my already frizzy hair into a mop.

April grabbed my arm and pulled me inside. "Trish. I'm glad to see you. Just so I can talk to someone who makes sense. Can you stay and have coffee?"

I shook my head. "I'm sorry. I have to get these things over to the high school."

Her smile died. "This place is just creepy. I hate it here." She glanced around. "I get out as much as possible. I left Granny Nettie here for a little while this morning to go pick up a costume from Connie's storage unit. Granny can stay by herself for an hour or so."

"I want a tuna sandwich," a voice called from the parlor.

A flicker of irritation flashed over April's face. "Granny, it's too early to eat." April looked at me. "She eats all the time. No wonder Connie gambled and Georgia acted like she did. And this house — I've never been anywhere in my life that's so gloomy. There are so many weird noises."

"Old houses are like that." I took a deep breath and wondered why I could still smell Connie's perfume.

"Well, it's weird. Like that —"

I heard one of the noises she was talking about — a distant, metallic-sounding noise. "I know what that is. Sherry was looking around last time she was here and said the hinges on the garden shed squeal. I'll bet the door is blowing in the wind."

Nettie shuffled out of the parlor. "I'm hungry." She noticed me standing there. "Is that Trish?"

April turned to her. "Yes. Trish Cunning-ham."

Nettie peered at me. "You were here before. Connie isn't here. She was packing to go, and they came and got her. But sometimes I still hear her."

April rolled her eyes. "I'll go get the costumes for you. I've got them folded in a bag."

She walked down the hall and disappeared into the back of the house. Nettie watched her for a minute then turned back to me. "People shouldn't yell. I taught the girls better than that. I'm glad you're not yelling."

"Who's been yelling at you?" I couldn't imagine April raising her voice.

Nettie shook her head. "Connie and that other woman. Georgia's friend. Did you know Connie was packing to leave?"

April returned with a bag. "I'll carry this to the car for you." She turned to Nettie. "You stay here. I'll be right back."

"What is Nettie talking about . . . people yelling?" I asked while I held open the passenger side door of my SUV.

April dropped the bag on the seat and shut the door. "I have no idea. I don't know half of what she's talking about. I guess Connie was arguing with someone." She sighed. "I miss working. Being here is driving me up the wall. Connie got out of jail this morning, but she won't be coming back here right now. I don't know what the family is going to do."

"How come she's out of jail if she stole Nettie's things?"

"The family isn't going to press charges. And most of the stuff has been recovered. They just want her to get some help with her gambling addiction."

"So they don't think she killed Georgia?"

April shrugged. "She says she didn't, but you'd better believe I'm not eating or drinking anything that I didn't bring here myself." She met my gaze. "I'm worried about being poisoned."

That reminded me of my earlier conversation with the nurse at my doctor's office. "Does Nettie take any medications for her heart?"

April nodded. "A beta-blocker."

"Is it called Inderal?"

"I can go inside and look," she said.

"Can you? And call me on my cell phone, okay? I need to get going or I'll be late."

When I arrived at the school, I parked in a side lot. As I got out of my car, Carla drove past me in her Volvo. That was odd. I thought that Sue, the school secretary, had said that Carla was leaving for vacation. And Sherry had just mentioned that Carla left this morning. I must have misunderstood.

Sherry was waiting by the side door to let me in. "Hey, Mrs. C. I'm glad you're here. Aunt Elissa just got here. Mr. Slade showed up at the door awhile ago, but I couldn't let him in. I'm under orders from Dad not to let anyone in except for you." She glanced at me with a happy grin. "Tommy talked to me for a little while before he went to work."

We passed through the double doors of the auditorium and walked down the red-carpeted aisle, then up the wooden stairs to the stage. Sherry held the red velvet side curtain back for me, and I walked past her into a wide space where Elissa sat in a molded plastic chair holding a clipboard, her cane hanging on the chair back. The two boxes of costumes we'd gotten from Connie the previous weekend were at her feet.

"Hi, Trish," she said.

We exchanged smiles, and I put my purse and bag on a table.

"We've been sorting through the costumes, checking them against the list Aunt Elissa got from Ms. Bickford." Sherry hung a suit on a hanger and slipped it onto one of two racks.

"Oh," I said. "I wonder how she got that. I thought Connie was supposed to get it from Marvin the day we found him in the band room . . . but, I guess she didn't."

Sherry picked up a man's dress jacket. "This is one of the things that Tommy is going to wear. Isn't it cool?"

I nodded, noting the proprietary way Sherry held the garment and spoke about my son.

Elissa smiled and shifted in her chair. Her cane clattered to the floor.

I picked it up and handed it to her. "Do you mind if I ask what happened?"

She shook her head. "Stupidity. I was running after a kid who had stolen a car. I blew out my knee."

"Is it going to get better?"

She shrugged. "I hope so, but it's a long process."

We were interrupted by ringing from my cell phone. It was April.

"Trish? Sorry. Everything's going crazy. Connie is missing."

"What?"

"Yeah. Anyway, that medicine? You were right about it. It's called Inderal."

"Thanks," I said. "Be careful."

"I will. I gotta go take care of the garden shed. That noise is driving me crazy."

I folded my phone shut and shoved it back into my purse, then glanced up at Sherry and Elissa. "Did you guys know Connie was in jail, but she was let out this morning, and now no one can find her?"

"Yeah," Sherry said. "Aunt Elissa told me

a little while ago."

"That means all the suspects from my list are on the loose. I guess for once the high school is the safest place to be. Even Carla is gone. I saw her leaving the parking lot when I arrived. I guess she's leaving for her vacation." I frowned. "You know what? Something just occurred to me. Why is Carla allowed to go on vacation? Isn't she a suspect?"

Elissa nodded. "You're right. She shouldn't be allowed to go."

"I thought she was already gone," Sherry said as she reverently hung up Tommy's jacket. "She took off at lunch today from what I heard."

Elissa glanced at her watch then handed her niece a black jacket. Sherry slipped her arms into the sleeves and twirled around. "This is the one that I'm going to wear in the scenes where I'm dressed to go on my honeymoon with Mortimer Brewster. Isn't it great? You know, we get to kiss at the end, when he carries me off the stage."

I ignored that and began to pull things out of the bag I'd gotten from April. Then Elissa's phone rang, and she yanked it from her pocket.

"Yes?" She listened for a moment then said yes again and hung up. "Listen, ladies.

I've got to go do something for a few minutes. I'll be back." She turned to Sherry. "You have your cell phone?"

She patted her pocket. "Was that Dad?"

Elissa nodded. "I'll be calling you to make sure you're all right."

She turned and disappeared through the curtain as Sherry hung the black suit up on the rack. "I know she's helping Dad. Maybe they've found Connie." She turned and faced me. "Did you know that Dad was going to meet that book author today for coffee?"

I looked up at her. "Abbie? Really?"

"Yeah. He likes her, I think. I like that she writes books." Sherry was very still, watching my face.

"I think she likes him, too."

"Do you know her well?"

I smiled. "Yep. She's my best friend."

Sherry relaxed. "Well, in that case, she must be all right."

My smile widened. "That's a nice thing to say." I turned and pulled a garment from the bag I'd gotten from April and held it out. It was a familiar-looking blue linen jacket. "This doesn't look like a costume."

Sherry reached out and touched it. "Smells like perfume."

She was right. It smelled like Connie's

distinctive scent. "I don't think this should be here."

Sherry grabbed the bottom of the jacket and held it out to look at it. Something rattled in the pocket. She reached inside and pulled out a folded piece of paper.

My mind snapped back to the day Georgia was murdered. Connie had been wearing this jacket and slipped a folded piece of paper into her pocket. She'd also looked scared. "What does that say?" I asked.

Sherry glanced through it. "It's an e-mail from that guy who died. You know the one in the article you and Aunt Elissa found? He says his family is coming around to the idea that he wants to marry Connie. He wants her to move back to Charlottesville to live."

I heard footsteps on the stairs to the stage. Elissa was back.

"Oh wow." Sherry gazed at me with wide eyes. "Then he says that Carla had been to see him and accused him of giving Connie a family heirloom watch that should have been hers."

The puzzle pieces fell together. I knew who the murderer was. I just didn't know why.

"What's his name?" I asked

The curtain moved and swung aside. I

looked up, expecting to see Elissa. Instead, Carla Bickford stood there.

"His name was Aaron Bryant," she said. "Ronnie."

21

Sherry and I were frozen in place.

"Well, I'm glad I came back to check on things," Carla said. "I couldn't find you at home, Trish."

"You were looking for me?"

She just smiled and held out her hand. "I'll take that paper, please."

Sherry glanced at me with raised brows, and I nodded. Carla snatched the letter from Sherry's outstretched hand, balled it up, and stuck it in her pocket, then stared at her. "I knew you were snooping around the school." I watched in horrified disbelief as she took a gun from her pocket and pointed it in our direction.

"I don't understand," Sherry said. "Are you the one who killed Georgia?"

"Not on purpose, but it's just as well. She had turned against me. The day before she died, she actually had the nerve to tell me that I was crazy."

She waved the gun at us, and I thought Georgia's words weren't too far from the mark.

Sherry's phone rang. Carla jumped. "Don't even think about getting that," she said.

"Sherry is a cop's daughter," I said. "You kill her, and he'll be after you the rest of your life."

She shrugged. "They won't know it's me. They all think I'm on vacation."

"No, they don't," Sherry said. "Aunt Elissa knows that Trish saw you in the parking lot."

Carla narrowed her eyes. "Then I guess Trish will be mistaken, won't she?" She glanced at me. "And your mother knows I was leaving. I stopped to get coffee."

"I don't think they'll believe you," I said.

"Sure they will. You'll be dead, so no one can argue with me. You are going to leave a note saying the two of you have gone out to Connie's house to return this jacket and pick up something. There, Connie is going to kill you two and kill herself. I intended to kill her to begin with, anyway."

"You wanted Connie to die?" I asked.

"Of course. She took what was mine — Ronnie."

Sherry watched us with huge eyes. "How

did Georgia die?"

"I bought coffee for the three of us and doctored Connie's with Inderal." Carla smiled as though she were proud of herself. "Both of them always drank those herbal concoctions with lots of ginseng, which was giving Connie heart palpitations. She also had low blood pressure. I figured the Inderal would finish her off. I wanted Kent Smith to be blamed. Unfortunately for Georgia, she drank Connie's coffee, as well as her own."

"Why blame Coach Smith?" Sherry breathed.

"Because he was threatening me. We were supposed to be working together. Now, that's enough!" Carla waved the gun at us. "One of you get a piece of paper."

Sherry turned and pulled a spiral notebook from her backpack. My mind was whirling.

"Write the note," Carla ordered Sherry.

"So this is all because of Aaron?" I asked.

Carla smiled bitterly. "He was mine. She took him. I thought when she moved here she'd lose interest. Then he'd take me back."

Sherry finished writing the note.

"Let me see." Carla held the gun on me while she read the note. "Okay. Put it on the table."

Sherry obeyed; then Carla held the curtain back so we could walk through.

"Where is Connie now?" I asked, trying to figure out how to get away.

"Right where I left her."

I felt a sharp twinge in my abdomen. A contraction. I doubled over to give myself more time to think.

"Get up," Carla ordered.

"Can't. Starting labor."

She swore. "I'll just have to shoot both of you here then plant the gun on Connie, which I was going to do, anyway. Then she'll be guilty of four murders."

My ploy wasn't working. Maybe I could talk us out of this. Appeal to Carla's mercy for the life of my baby and for Sherry. I slowly stood and glanced at Sherry, whose face was ashen. Then I realized what Carla had said.

"Four murders?"

Carla smiled. "My dearest Ronnie. He was shot with this gun."

My heart thumped. If she could kill someone she loved, there would be no appealing to her mercy.

"My aunt will be back any minute," Sherry said.

"No, she won't." Carla smiled.

"What did you do to her?" I asked, thinking the worst.

"I watched her drive out of the parking lot. I called in an anonymous emergency call. I told them Connie is threatening Marvin — at his house across town. I knew she was helping the cops."

Prickles of anger began to replace my fear. No way was I going to let some monster truck principal kill us.

I met Sherry's gaze and narrowed my eyes at her. She did the same. That's when I knew we would figure out something.

Carla held the curtain aside, keeping her gun trained on us. "Let's go. Close together, please."

The phone in my purse began to ring. Carla jumped, but it didn't distract her. Then Sherry's phone began to ring in her pocket. Perfect. In the cacophony of noise, Carla's gaze and aim wavered just long enough for me to slam her gun arm. Then Sherry slugged Carla in the stomach with a strength that surprised me. The gun clattered to the floor.

Carla lost her balance and fell. But she recovered quickly and scrabbled on the floor for the gun. I kicked it to the back of the stage. Sherry tackled Carla and knocked her to her back.

Carla screamed like a banshee and tried

to get up. Sherry boxed her ear then pulled her hair, making her scream louder.

I couldn't believe my eyes. My son had picked the perfect girl.

Suddenly, the doors to the auditorium flew open and cops overran the place. Detective Scott sprinted down the aisle, followed by Corporal Fletcher, who surprised me by how fast he could move. Another deputy leaped up on the stage and handcuffed Carla. Elissa followed behind them, limping on her cane.

"Are you both okay?" Detective Scott yelled as he ran up the stage stairs. "We called Sherry twice. Then Trish. I was frantic when neither of you answered your phones."

"We're fine, Daddy," Sherry said.

"Fletcher, take care of Trish," the detective said as he snatched Sherry into his arms.

The stage was swarming with cops.

Another pain seized my abdomen. I grabbed at the plastic chair and sat down hard.

Corporal Fletcher rushed to my side. "Mrs. C., you don't look so good. Did she hurt you?"

"No." I grimaced in pain. "But I am going to have a baby."

22

"I love you." Max leaned over my hospital bed and kissed my cheek.

I brushed my fingers over his lips. "Ditto."

He glanced at the bassinet next to my bed. "Rest, now. I'm sure Chris will wake up hungry soon."

After one last kiss, he left the room. I watched him, remembering what Shirl had said — how women liked to watch his . . . Well, she was right. He looked *good.* And I vowed to get back into good shape now that the pregnancy was over.

For once, I was grateful to be in the hospital. I stared at my new son. Despite his early arrival, he was healthy. Delivery had been easy compared to the pregnancy.

From the corner of my eye, I saw a shadow at the door and looked up. Connie and Marvin were standing there. She was holding a present.

I was surprised to see them. "Come in."

"I . . . we . . . came by to thank you," Connie said as they walked softly across the room. She handed me the present and peered into the bassinet. "He's beautiful."

"Thank you." I laid the box on the bed next to me. I wasn't sure what to say after that. "Um, Marvin, what happened to you in the band room? It was a heart attack, right?"

"Yes. All the stress. It wasn't a murder attempt."

"So you're going to stop eating doughnuts?"

He grinned. "Yes."

We were all silent for a few moments.

Connie shifted. "I guess you're wondering why we're here."

"Yes. I am."

She and Marvin glanced at each other.

"We wanted to thank you," Connie repeated. "You saved my life. You told April about the shed door hinges squealing, and the detective said you helped him with some of your observations."

That was news to me. He'd been by to visit and so had Corporal Fletcher, but I guessed neither had said anything because I hadn't been in shape for a discussion at the time.

"I don't know the whole story about the shed."

"Carla had me tied up in there but didn't fasten the door tight. In all that wind, it blew open. When April came out to shut it, she found me. I told the cops on the phone that Carla had gone to your house to get you. She thought you'd be home resting, not helping Elissa and Sherry."

I glanced at Chris and shivered to think how close we'd come to being killed. "Connie, did you know it was Carla?"

"I wasn't sure. I couldn't figure out why she would have killed Georgia. But remember when you told me about the watch?"

I nodded.

"That's when I wondered if Carla had stolen it from Aaron after I gave it to him to have it fixed. But I couldn't go to the police because I was afraid they would blame me for Aaron's murder or something." She paused. "You know what the really horrible thing is?"

I shook my head.

"Georgia and I were together in the band room before she died. We had the coffee that Carla brought us. I couldn't drink mine because I was having heart palpitations, so Georgia drank both cups. We were fighting. She'd found out I was gambling, and she saw what I was doing in the library the day before. She said she'd told Marvin, but he didn't believe her."

Marvin put his arm around her.

"I was so angry with her I stormed out." She swallowed and began to cry. "If I had stayed, I might have been able to call the paramedics in time to save her."

"I'm pretty sure by the time she was having convulsions, it would have been too late," Marvin said.

I looked at him. "Why did Georgia tell you about Connie gambling?"

"She was angry and wanted someone to stop Connie. She thought I could."

This must have been the argument that Karen talked about when she wanted me to solve the murder.

Connie sighed. "Most everything I stole has been recovered." She glanced shyly at Marvin. "He went and got them back. The family is willing to let me take care of Granny Nettie again if I attend classes for my addiction."

I turned to Marvin. "Why aren't you in jail? I thought you were part of the drug and cheating scheme."

He shook his head. "No. Unfortunately, though, I'm the one who gave the idea to Coach Smith. At least about the Inderal."

He reddened. "I used to take it to help me perform in concerts. One day I was joking with him that we ought to use it to try to improve the kids' concentration during tests. He took me seriously. And he got Carla involved. She was always out to prove herself. She wanted to move on to a more prestigious school."

"So why were you afraid that day at the football game?"

"Because I was working with the cops to set up Coach Smith, and I was afraid if I talked to him for long, he'd know something was up."

"Oh." My eyelids felt heavy.

"We should let you sleep," Connie said.

I forced my eyes to focus. "Wait a minute. I have two more questions. Marvin, why were you at Self-Storage that day? And why did you get mad at the dry cleaners?"

He laughed. "You are thorough, aren't you?" He glanced at Connie. "When I picked up the dry cleaning as a favor to Connie — trying to get her to notice me — the girl there gave me some papers she'd found in the pockets of a jacket. One of them was a pawn shop receipt. Then I knew that what Georgia had said about Connie was true." His cheeks reddened. "I managed to steal a self-storage key from Connie's house to see if I could find any evidence in her unit of her stealing stuff from Nettie. I did."

"So the cops knew?" I asked.

Connie nodded. "Yes. That's how the family found out."

My eyelids were drooping again. "I'm sorry. I have to nap."

"We understand," Connie said.

I heard their footsteps as they left the room, and I smiled. I love a happy ending.

Two days later, I was sitting in the living room with Chris in my arms. Max was fixing dinner with Karen's help. Tommy, along with Sherry, was helping Sammie with a school project. I was actually enjoying doing nothing, even though I was still sore and tired from the baby's birth. But my brain was doing fine. I had my clue notebook next to me, and I was going over my questions and observations. I needed one more answer before I would be satisfied.

When the doorbell rang, Charlie, as usual, raced to get it.

"Mom!" He yelled. "It's that policeman guy again. And Abbie."

This was a pleasant surprise.

Detective Scott and Abbie walked into the

living room, and she made a beeline for Chris.

"He's so adorable," she murmured.

Detective Scott smiled at me. "Congratulations, again."

"Thank you. What are you guys up to? You know Sherry's here, right?" I was worried that he would still object to Sherry and Tommy being together.

"Yes," he said. "It's fine."

"We were out shopping," Abbie said. "We've been invited for dinner. Max wanted to surprise you."

"It *is* a surprise. Especially since you're together."

Detective Scott glanced at her then back at me. "Yes. I guess I have you and Fletcher to thank for that."

I narrowed my eyes. "You need to remember something, Detective. Abbie is one of the most important people in my life. I used to beat kids up in school to protect her."

He grinned at my mock threat. "I don't think you'll have to worry."

"I guess this means you're one of the family now."

"In that case, how about you call me Eric?"

I wasn't sure I could get used to that.

He noticed my notebook. "Still thinking?"

"Yes." I picked it up. "I have one unanswered question."

"Let me see if I can take care of that." He dropped into a chair opposite me and stretched out his legs. He was the most relaxed I'd ever seen him. Abbie sat in the other chair.

"Just like that? I don't have to beg or coerce you?"

"No," he said. "Ask away. I owe you. It was two of your clues that helped me nail Carla."

"Which ones?"

"The one about Carla's fiancé and the one about the watch. The cops in Charlottesville were able to pin Aaron Bryant's murder on her, as well."

"Wow." I felt like I'd been given a gold medal.

Abbie winked at me.

I settled back on the couch. "So you asked Marvin to set the coach up to be caught?"

"Yes, we did. That was the only way we could get to him. Have him think Marvin finally agreed to help. One of the kids told Marvin what was going on. When Marvin confronted Coach Smith, he threatened he'd tell law enforcement that the drugs were Marvin's idea. And Carla would back

Coach Smith up, so Marvin came to us first."

I glanced down at my notebook. "I think that's about it. I understand everything else."

"Okay." Eric smiled at me then turned to Abbie. "Why don't I leave the two of you here to talk? I've got a little gift for my daughter." He smiled broadly as he walked away.

"She's in the family room," I said. When he was gone, I turned to Abbie. "What is it?"

"A charm bracelet. He's going to document their life together with charms."

"That is the sweetest thing in the whole world," I said. "He's much more sentimental and sensitive than I thought."

"No." She laughed. "He's not."

I grinned. "Ah. It was your idea."

"Yes, but he thinks it was his, so let's leave it that way."

Abbie was learning fast.

Max walked into the room. "Time to eat."

Abbie stood. "Why don't you let me carry my godson to the dinner table?" She took Chris from my arms and walked from the room.

Max held out his hand, took one of mine, and helped me to my feet. "Have I told you how much I love you?"

"A couple hundred times, I think."

He kissed my forehead. "I have the last few months to make up for."

"You're not the only one," I murmured. I was determined to practice the lesson the Lord had taught me — walking in love.

I picked up my notebook as we left the room. I would retire it with the empty ones in the kitchen drawer.

Max grabbed my hand. "You're not sad it's over, are you?"

"Are you kidding?" I glanced up at him. "I've got enough to do now that Chris has been born. I might just give up my sleuthing hobby."

Max met my gaze with a tiny grin. "Right. And pigs fly."

ABOUT THE AUTHOR

Candice Speare lives in Maryland surrounded by cornfields and cattle. She spends most days in her second story office in the company of Winston the African gray parrot. Candice is the author of one published book, *Murder in the Milk Case,* the first in the Trish Cunningham series. Besides plotting fictional murder and mayhem, she is an amateur photographer and fiddles with digital images. She also dabbles in Web site design. When she has the time, she likes to garden, scrapbook, sew, and play the piano — especially worship music. She loves to collect recipes and on occasion has even been known to remove one from the file drawer and make it. Rumors of her eccentricities are true. Please visit her Web site at www.candicemillerspeare.com where you can read her blog and find out more information about contests for her readers,

as well as upcoming events and new re-
leases.

The employees of Thorndike Press hope you have enjoyed this Large Print book. All our Thorndike, Wheeler, and Kennebec Large Print titles are designed for easy reading, and all our books are made to last. Other Thorndike Press Large Print books are available at your library, through selected bookstores, or directly from us.

For information about titles, please call:
(800) 223-1244

or visit our Web site at:
http://gale.cengage.com/thorndike

To share your comments, please write:
Publisher
Thorndike Press
295 Kennedy Memorial Drive
Waterville, ME 04901